A Second Chance in Bent Creek

Harker Brothers Ranch Book 1

Catie Cahill

Contents

Come Home to Bent Creek

A SMALL TOWN IN Montana where everyone knows everyone, secrets live in the shadows of the mountains, and love is just waiting to be found. One by one, the Harker brothers return home to reclaim their ranch, face their family's past troubles with the Nobles, and find the love they didn't know they needed.

Chapter One

Larkin

Three days.

That's how long Nick Harker was back in Bent Creek before I heard anything about it. Mrs. Young, who knows everything about everyone before they even know it themselves, let it slip while she was ordering her small decaf.

I was still mulling over whether I was annoyed or happy that I didn't know first when Marybeth Noble slipped through the door of Mountain Roasters. There were only a couple of customers at tables, drinking their coffee and eating scones and muffins. I smiled at Marybeth, glad to have my best friend as a distraction from the thoughts whirling around my head.

"Isn't it spring yet?" Marybeth said as she rubbed her gloved hands together.

I grabbed the to-go mug she'd set on the counter and began to fill it with today's light roast blend. "Shouldn't you be wishing for winter to last forever?" Marybeth ran Bent Creek Christmas, an adorable shop just down the street filled with everything Christmas.

My two-year-old, Diego, thought Marybeth's shop was basically Santa's home when he wasn't at the North Pole.

She made a face. "People can buy ornaments and stockings in warm weather too."

But even as she said it, I knew she wished the Christmas season were longer. Bent Creek Christmas was barely hanging on, and Marybeth worried constantly about how she'd see the shop through summer.

"Are those made by the best baker in town?" She pointed at the frosted blueberry scones in the bakery case.

"You mean Mrs. Foley?" I joked, although Mrs. Foley definitely had me beat in baked goods, simply by the number of years she'd been at it.

Marybeth rolled her eyes at me.

"No. I wish." I looked at the case longingly. I'd asked my boss more than once if I could use the kitchen in back to bake something to sell. He shot me down every time.

"Just keep at him. Maybe slip him one of those chocolate-chip cookies the next time you make some."

"I guess." Time to change the subject—away from my inability to convince Charlie that I could be more than a barista with childcare problems, to the one thing I couldn't get off my mind this morning. "Mrs. Young came in earlier today."

Marybeth paused, an open packet of Splenda held over her mug, sympathy filling her eyes. "Nick," she said softly.

She knew. I ignored the tiny sting in the corner of my heart that said everyone must have known except me. "How did you find out?"

Marybeth grimaced as she crumpled the empty packet and dropped it into the trash can. "He went to see Gabe."

Her words eased the bruise around my heart. Of course Nick would visit his stepbrother, who happened to be Marybeth's boyfriend.

"Did he say why he was back in town?" I hated myself for wanting to know. I shouldn't care, not after what he'd done. But I couldn't *not* ask.

Marybeth leaned a hip against the counter and eyed me over the top of her mug. I knew she was searching for signs of that mangled part of me that Nick had left behind eleven years ago. But she didn't need to worry. I'd had my heart broken again since then, and that raw part of it was covered with a pretty thick scar by now.

Marybeth sighed. "Gabe asked him. He's hoping Nick can help him figure out how to buy the ranch back."

I nodded. It made sense. I just wasn't prepared for the past to come roaring back like the rain after a drought.

"I don't know *how* Gabe thinks Nick can help him. He's gotten nowhere trying to figure out what this Chestnut Moon company is or how to reach them," Marybeth said.

I reached for the rag I kept below the counter, just for something to occupy my hands. "Well, if anyone can help him, it's Nick." They were the same age and were inseparable in high school. Both on the football team, same group of friends, always at the same parties, and the best of friends.

But they weren't the same person. Where Gabe was light, Nick was dark. He was the realist to Gabe's optimism. But he'd been unfailingly loyal to anyone who'd earned his trust—family, of course. Friends. And me. Until everything he knew turned upside down.

And then he was gone.

"Larkin?" Marybeth's concerned voice yanked me back to the present.

"I'm fine," I said quickly as I scrubbed at the already clean countertop with the rag. A quick glance at her told me she didn't believe a word I said.

"Well, if he deigns to speak to me, I'll tell him off for you. I've been dying to do that for eleven years," she said.

I bit back a smile. Marybeth would do it, too. I had no doubt. "Please tell me he hasn't been rude to you."

"Not exactly. I've only seen him once, when he was meeting up with Gabe. He didn't say anything, but . . ." Marybeth paused, her eyes on the lid of her mug. "It was clear exactly how he feels about me being with his brother."

My heart ached for my friend. I dropped the rag back under the counter and reached for Marybeth's arm. "He'll have to get over it." I gave her arm a squeeze, and she looked up at me with a sad smile.

"I don't know why they *care* so much. Nick. Luke." She shook her head, as if she could simply cast off the history between her family and the Harkers. Her brother Luke had made his opinion on her relationship with Gabe awfully clear from the start. "It's the past. What's done is done. Why can't they just move on?"

"I don't know," I said honestly. Even as Nick's girlfriend back in high school, I'd always been on the periphery. I never wanted to know more, even after the night I almost lost my life because of it. "Maybe if Gabe can get the ranch back, it'll help heal some of that."

Marybeth shrugged. "Sometimes I worry it'll just make things worse." She shook her head again. "I'm sorry, Larkin. Here I was trying to support you, and I'm focusing on my problems instead."

"No apologies, okay?" I gave her a smile.

"Okay. Where's Diego today?"

Nothing could lighten my mood like talking about Diego. "With Mom. She's got Tuesdays off now."

I chatted with Marybeth for a few more minutes about Mom's new job at the hospital and Diego's recent obsession with toy cars. When she left to go open her shop, the nervous energy I'd had ever since Mrs. Young had stopped in hummed through my veins.

By the time my shift was over, Mountain Roasters was sparkling clean—and I'd made up my mind.

I filled a cup with a teaspoon of sugar and dark roast coffee, and tossed a few dollars into the till so I wouldn't have Charlie breathing down my neck. I shot off a quick text to Mom telling her I'd be a little late. And then I drove to the broken down old motel by the interstate, several miles outside of town.

I was going to get Nick Harker out of my head. And the only way to do that was to get this reunion out of the way.

Chapter Two

Nick

THE SLOPE MOTEL LOOKED almost respectable in daylight.

Almost.

I shut the truck door and zipped up my coat. This place was a freezing wasteland, and I couldn't wait to get out of it and back to Texas, where I could breathe without the past and the cold burning my lungs. Why Gabe was so hell-bent on staying here was beyond me.

The Harkers were done. Scattered. Over. Most people would say that was for the best.

And maybe it was.

I was halfway to the questionable warmth of my room when I realized I needed to pay up if I was staying here past tonight. And as much as I wanted to jump in my truck and hightail it back down south, I couldn't do that to Gabe.

Biting back a curse at both Gabe's stubbornness and my own sense of loyalty, I turned and headed back toward the motel's office. I yanked open the door, ready to feel the heat warming my bones despite the fact that it would cost me more of my hard-earned cash.

But instead of the blast of heat I expected, I got a girl.

She stumbled right into me, and I grabbed her arms to keep her from falling as something warm splashed from the cup in her hand. Droplets hit my face as most of it spilled down my coat, soaking into my jeans and pooling onto my boots.

"Oh, no! I'm s—" Her voice caught.

And I realized who she was the same second that recognition dawned in her brown eyes.

The door clunked shut behind her, and there I was, holding Larkin Reyes in my arms as if the past eleven years had never happened.

I let go of her just as her mouth opened. She closed it without saying a word. And yet somehow all I wanted was to hear her say my name again.

Not that I deserved it.

"I . . ." Larkin began, not meeting my eyes. And then she began dabbing at my coat with a crumpled tissue she'd pulled from her pocket. "Sorry."

The seconds ticked by loudly in my head as Larkin pressed the tissue against my coat. Somewhere on the interstate behind the motel, a truck's Jake Brake tore through the low rumble of traffic. Larkin shoved the soaked tissue into her coat pocket and held out the half-full coffee cup.

"I brought this for you."

I blinked at it as if I'd never seen coffee in my life. "You brought me coffee?" I said stupidly as I took the cup from her.

She shrugged, as if it weren't any big deal at all. Was it?

"I work there. Mountain Roasters." She pointed to the cup.

"I know."

She looked up at me sharply, and I wished I could take the words back. "Gabe told me."

She nodded, seemingly appeased that I wasn't creeping around and checking up on her. Like she hadn't been on my mind from the second Gabe called me back in Texas and asked me to come up here.

"Marybeth told me he wants you to help him buy the ranch."

Marybeth. The spilled coffee had turned cold in the denim against my legs, and I focused on that sensation as I schooled my expression into something neutral. Marybeth was a nice enough girl, Larkin's best friend for as long as I could remember.

And she was a Noble.

My face might have remained expressionless, but the coffee cup bent under my hand. Larkin's gaze flickered toward it.

"Are you going to?" she asked quickly, looking back up at me.

My mind churned slowly from vengeance to escape to memories of the way those chocolate eyes used to watch me with nothing but love.

"Help Gabe?" she prodded when I didn't get there fast enough.

I snorted. "We'll see." Buying the ranch was a dead end, but forcing him to get his head on straight about Marybeth Noble was something I could help with.

I took a sip of the cooled coffee. Bitter and sweet, just as I liked it. I caught Larkin's eyes, surprised she'd remembered.

"I don't forget," she said as she read my mind. And for a second I wondered if she'd meant more than coffee.

Shame burned my insides. What I'd done to her years ago wasn't right. And it was a miracle she hadn't thrown the coffee in my face. Instead she'd brought it to me, like some kind of peace offering I didn't deserve.

She glanced out at the narrow parking lot that was surrounded by dirty snowbanks. "I need to go." She stopped speaking abruptly, almost as if she'd cut off something now unsaid. Maybe *Good to see you* or some other kind end to a conversation. Except it probably wasn't good to see me. And she had no reason to be kind.

"My mom is waiting," she said instead.

A corner of my brain lit up, like a light bulb in an old Bugs Bunny cartoon. Gabe had mentioned a kid, a little boy whose coward father had split town the moment he'd found out.

I grabbed hold of Larkin's arm just before she stepped away. I knew it was a mistake, but I didn't care. It might have been my imagination, or maybe some long-forgotten memory, but I could feel the warmth of her skin through her coat. She drew in a breath, and for a second, it was like no time had passed. We were still in high school, and I was just about to pull her in for a goodbye kiss that would last longer than it should. Then she would laugh against my lips and gently push me away.

But reality came crashing down around me as she lifted confused eyes to my face. She frowned slightly, and I dropped my hand.

"What's his name?" I asked. "Your son?"

Her mouth curved up into the ghost of a smile. "Diego."

I returned her smile, genuinely glad that his presence in her life gave her joy. Without another word, she turned away again and began walking across the parking lot toward a Kia that had seen better days. I wondered how she kept that thing on the road all winter as she slipped inside and started it up.

She didn't look back as she left, but I stood there, coffee growing cold in the cup and on my jeans.

Leaving Larkin Reyes had been the worst mistake of my life.

Chapter Three

Larkin

I WAS STILL SHAKING when I pulled into the driveway of the rental house Diego and I shared with Mom. I sat for a moment after I turned the car off, trying to steady my breathing and force Nick Harker from my mind.

But it was impossible.

Just being near him consumed all of my senses, same as it had years ago. I hadn't expected that. I was so much older now. A mom. And the anger and loneliness I'd felt after he left had been nicely tucked away in a long-forgotten corner of my mind.

But the second I'd laid eyes on him, every emotion I'd ever had about Nick had come rushing back in a deluge. It had taken all my self-control to even speak normally to him. And when he'd held on to steady me . . . and grabbed my arm as if he didn't want me to leave . . .

I drew in a shuddering breath and let it out, the air fogging the cooling windshield. Why did he still have that effect on me? It had been so long. I'd been through my share of heartbreak and was still standing.

Seeing Nick shouldn't have me reduced to a nervous, shaking mess.

I gathered my purse and reluctantly left the car. If I didn't go in soon, Mom would start to wonder what was wrong. And Diego's sweet face was already pressed to the window.

I waved at him and he grinned. He disappeared immediately, leaving fingerprints on the window as he raced to the side door.

The door opened the second I walked up to it, and Diego rushed into my arms.

"Mama!" He pressed his face into my legs.

My heart soared. Diego was the best part of any day. I scooped him up and gave him a squeeze until he pushed against me. I set him back down to run through the kitchen and back to the living room.

"How was he?" I asked Mom as I set down my purse and hung up my coat.

"Fine." Mom leaned a hip against the oven door. "He decided he loves green beans. That's all he wanted for lunch."

"At least it's something healthy." I could feel her eyes on me as I thumbed through the mail on the countertop. Nothing got past Jeanine Reyes. And I knew it was better to face the situation head-on rather than hide it.

I sighed and tapped my fingers against the envelopes as I turned to face her. "I saw Nick. Nick Harker." Like she'd ever forget him and the damage he'd caused.

Her eyebrows lifted into her sideswept blonde bangs. We were a pair, Mom and I. We didn't even look related, thanks to my father's Mexican heritage. But we were both petite, and our eyes were the same, dark brown and serious. Hers pinned me down now, waiting for more.

I swallowed and shoved my hands into my jeans pockets, summoning all that old anger and sadness instead of the feel of Nick's hands on my arms, or the way those blue-gray eyes seemed to see into my soul.

"He's in town. Something to do with his brother. I thought I'd get it out of the way."

"And?"

I sucked in a huff. "Nothing. He'll probably be gone in a week." I didn't know that, of course, but how long could it take him to figure out what Marybeth already knew? It was going to be almost impossible to buy back that ranch, she'd said. "I'm sure he's got stuff to do in . . . wherever it is he came from." I had the strongest desire to know where Nick Harker lived these days. He dressed like he still lived here. Old jeans, boots, worn-in cowboy hat. Maybe he was living on a ranch somewhere. It felt right.

Mom was quiet a moment, pressing her lips together. "He got to you, didn't he?"

A wave of emotion rose inside me, and all I wanted to do was run to my mom and let her hold me while I cried. But I didn't. I couldn't let Nick make me feel like that again. He didn't deserve any more of my tears. So I took a deep breath, shoved down the old feelings that threatened to take me over, and shook my head. "I'm fine. I promise."

Mom's eyes narrowed slightly, and I knew she didn't believe me. But I had a son to take care of now. I couldn't let myself fall apart.

Nick Harker was my past. And that was exactly where he'd stay.

"Look, Mama!" Diego ran on his short little legs back into the kitchen, clutching a piece of paper in his hands. He handed it to me, and I smiled as I looked at it. Mom had drawn something that looked like a car, and Diego had attempted to color it in with a garish purple and red.

"It's beautiful, baby." I squatted down to give him a kiss on his cheek.

He shrieked with glee and ran away again. I stood, keeping that little purple and red car in my hand as a reminder of what was important.

"You know," Mom said as she finally pushed away from the oven and opened a cabinet. "I met the nicest young doctor at work yesterday. He just came here from New York. I asked around, and the other nurses said he was single."

"*Mom*. No." I made sure to catch her eye before I bent down to retrieve a cookie sheet. I needed to bake. That would help me get my mind straight.

"Are you sure?" She looked pained that I wouldn't even consider letting her set me up. "He was awfully nice. Smart, too."

Of course he was smart. He was a doctor. "I'm sure."

She tucked away her disappointment quickly, but not before I caught it. I reached out as I set the cookie sheet on the counter. "Thank you, Mom. I know you're just looking out for me." I squeezed her arm, and she smiled at me.

"I just want you to be happy, Larkin baby."

"I know. And I am. I have you and Diego. I have Marybeth. And my job is mostly okay."

Mom laughed at that. Given how much I complained about Charlie, she probably thought I completely hated Mountain Roasters. But it wasn't bad, most of the time. Charlie was a pain, but when he wasn't there, I actually liked the place. It was nice to see people every day and chat with them.

"Do me a favor, though." She tucked a stray piece of hair behind my ear. "Stay away from Nick."

She didn't have to ask me twice. "I will."

Her phone buzzed. She picked it up from the counter and groaned. "This new nurse's aide is going to make me crazy. She's constantly asking me to cover her shifts." Her fingers flew over the screen as she texted.

I turned my attention to checking the dinner she'd started making and then mixing up dough for sugar cookies. Measuring and mixing took all my attention, driving the day's worries to the back of my mind. It was exactly what I needed.

After dinner and a cookie more than she'd meant to eat, Mom turned in early to be ready for a twelve-hour day at the hospital in the morning, and I took a long time putting Diego to bed. When he couldn't keep his eyes open any longer, I kissed him goodnight, turned out his light, and pulled the door partially closed.

The house was strangely quiet. I could have turned on the TV and scrolled through my phone. That would have been the perfect distraction. But instead, I stepped outside.

The snow-covered gravel in the driveway crunched under my shoes as I wrapped my arms around myself. I should've put on a coat, but the craving for the cold, fresh air had gotten the better of me.

Staring up at the clear sky, I scanned the stars as if they held some sort of answer. I hadn't lied to Mom. I *was* happy—mostly. But seeing Nick had stirred something inside of me. Something restless but wary. Some deep kind of longing I hadn't known was there.

Why him? Why couldn't it have been Diego's father who'd come back to town? I'd thought Will Boden was the answer to my prayers when he showed up. But he'd broken my heart too, showing me exactly what kind of man he was when he left Diego to grow up without a dad. Seeing Will again would've made me angry—but that was all.

There wouldn't have been this rush of confusing emotions I didn't know how to stop.

A noise from the street drew my attention away from the sky. My teeth chattered as a truck drove slowly by. It was time to go inside before some neighbor asked Mom if I was all right, standing out in the freezing cold at night with no coat.

As I stepped back inside the warmth of our small house, I realized the cold had made one thing clear—my focus needed to be on Diego. And getting myself all confused by the past wasn't good.

I would keep the past right where it was—for the future of my son.

Chapter Four

Nick

I AVOIDED IT FOR days. Until I couldn't anymore.

I sat back against the seat of my truck but kept one hand on the wheel. Maybe I needed the reassurance that I could leave at any time. Leave, instead of looking out to see what a wreck the old ranch had become.

I'd been right when Gabe first called me. This place was a bad investment, but not for the reasons I'd originally had.

Gabe had told me what to expect, but it was nothing compared to seeing it in person. A fresh blanket of snow had fallen overnight, and the white softened the effect of the neglected yard and corral, the slowly disintegrating barn, and the abandoned house.

I breathed out through my teeth. It was an embarrassment. Who would buy a place like this and let it rot? An unrestrained anger toward this Chestnut Moon company that owned the property rose up inside me. What the hell was wrong with these people? Before the law had caught up with Pops, this place was thriving. A few hundred head of cattle once called the Harker Ranch home, and it could've been more if Pops had bought up nearby land as it became available.

But Pops was always busy with other things.

I gripped the steering wheel like I could somehow cut off memories of the past. But they swirled and charged and refused to be ignored. People arriving in the dead of night. That warehouse-like garage Pops built off in the wooded area at the edge of our land. The gaping loss of Gabe's mom, who was a mother to all of us. My brief stint working for Pops at seventeen. Gunshots.

Fumbling for the handle, I threw open the door and jumped out. The cold air smacked away the bad memories as I looked up at the house. Despite the state of the place, I couldn't help but smile. It hadn't *all* been terrible. And if I was honest with myself, it was mostly good. It was just that the bad loomed so large in my mind sometimes that there was no space left to remember the good times.

I shoved my hands into my pockets and graced the undisturbed snow with my footprints. Larkin had loved the front porch, at least until that one night ruined it for her. We used to sit out there for hours, pretending all we were doing was holding hands whenever anyone walked by.

Larkin.

It would've been easier if she'd come to throw that coffee in my face. At least I'd understand that. Instead, she gave it to me like some kind of peace offering, when I was the one who owed her an apology that could never fully make up for what I'd done.

I didn't know what to make of it.

Kicking aside the snow, I uncovered some of the gravel that still lined the driveway. Some of the pieces had flecks of fool's gold, and Larkin used to shriek and scoop them up, declaring herself a billion-aire. It got to be a joke between us, and I smiled at the memory as the sun caught the shiny part of one of the stones. I reached down for it and brushed off the snow before dropping it into my pocket.

I might as well walk away from what remained of this place with at least one good memory.

Moving around the side of the house, I looked up automatically and found the window of the bedroom I'd shared with Gabe. The glass was still intact, and I could picture the room like I'd just been in there yesterday. How long did it take for memories like that to fade? Or would it stay as clear as it was now forever?

I made an entire circle of the house, the broken windows and splintered bits of wood piercing parts of my heart I thought had died years ago. I didn't dare look inside. I didn't know what I'd see, and I wasn't sure I wanted whatever was in there to overshadow the good memories. The outbuildings were all in various states of disrepair, with the barn in the worst shape of all. I peered inside, and the looming shapes of abandoned equipment stared back at me.

What a waste. It was *all* such a waste. The anger roiled up, scattering any sadness I'd indulged in. I clenched my hands into fists and fought the urge to hit the deteriorating wood of the barn.

Generations of Harkers had lived here, worked here, died here. And for what? For the Nobles to finally get what they wanted. For Pops to lose it all. For us to scatter across the country to pick up the pieces of our lives and try to make something new.

Half the time I didn't know if I was angry at Carson Noble or at Pops. And most of the time, I didn't care. Maverick tried for a while to get me to come to California and visit Pops in prison. At first I told him no. Then I ignored him. Now I don't remember the last time I talked to my youngest brother.

Because that's what the Nobles did to us. And how Gabe can even think about being with one of them . . .

Back at the truck, I slumped against the passenger door, looking out over the snow-covered, barren fields. Small trees grew up here and there, like nature was well on its way to reclaiming this place. Maybe it was for the best.

For half a second, as I'd walked around the house, I could see what Gabe hoped for. I could imagine the house, the barn, everything fixed up and full of people working and laughing and doing those everyday things that made life worth living.

But the reality is, the rot that came with the Nobles infected this place. Pops let it consume him as he channeled his grief over Mom and then Katina, Gabe's mom, into something dark and dangerous—until it destroyed all of us.

No. I clenched my fists as I forced my eyes past the house and the outbuildings toward the sky. We weren't destroyed. We were still here. Me, Gabe, my younger brothers. We still had lives to live—far away from Bent Creek. Gabe just needed reminding of that.

He needed to end this thing with Marybeth Noble before it was too late to get out. Before her brother Luke lost his patience and ended it for him. I'd never put an ounce of faith in Luke, not after what he'd done.

Unless . . .

The needles on the giant evergreen out front of the house waved as the chill breeze skittered across the empty property. It seemed so clear now, why Luke was tolerating this so-called relationship.

Because it might not be a relationship at all. Not if he put Marybeth up to it.

But why?

I turned abruptly toward the truck. I'd find out. Then I would end it and get myself and Gabe back out of this town.

Chapter Five

Marybeth

MRS. MCNEELY ALMOST DROPPED her hot chocolate when Nick Harker walked into my store.

No, *walked* was too bland a word. *Stormed* was a more appropriate description. The door slammed, and I flinched, half expecting to see suited-up executives from Gabe's old real estate firm in Chicago coming back to demand I sell the building to them. And poor Mrs. McNeely sloshed her peppermint hot chocolate down her coat at the sudden intrusion into Bent Creek Christmas.

My heart slowed when I saw it wasn't some disdainful real estate exec from Durnstorff & Vibert. As much as Nick didn't like me, at least he wasn't interested in buying my shop.

I stepped around the counter and handed Mrs. McNeely a paper towel before turning a smile toward Gabe's brother. "Hey, Nick."

All I got in return was a wary frown. "You have a minute?"

I glanced around my shop. Besides Mrs. McNeely, there was a family and an older couple from one of the nearby ski resorts. Bent

Creek Christmas desperately needed customers. "I'm sorry, but . . ." I gestured at the people in the shop.

"I'll wait."

He posted himself between the door and a display of Christmas-themed towels. In between helping the family choose an ornament and checking out Mrs. McNeely's purchase, I glanced at him. Arms crossed, hat tilted just so, he looked every inch the same boy who'd swept Larkin off her feet and then broken her heart. I was proud of her for facing him—and petrified he'd try to worm his way back into her heart.

He caught me looking at him and met my gaze with a stony expression. I sighed inwardly. I hadn't exactly expected any of Gabe's brothers to be overjoyed about us, but I suppose I'd hoped for something more than outright distaste.

"I never expected to see him back in town," Mrs. McNeely whispered across the counter. She'd been glancing back at him periodically, and I could only imagine he was getting used to those stares since stepping foot back in Bent Creek. Gabe had gotten looks like that too, until he stopped seeing the town as his enemy.

I waved goodbye to the older couple who followed Mrs. McNeely out the door. The woman glanced up at Nick, seemingly puzzled about his presence. Maybe if I stuck a Santa hat on Nick's head, he'd look a little less intimidating. Instead, he resembled some sort of cowboy bouncer, ready to evict any shopper who stepped out of line.

After ringing up the family's purchase of an ornament and some Christmas candy and seeing them out the door, I drew in a breath and began straightening the cups by the hot chocolate I kept for customers while I waited for Nick to speak.

"What's your brother up to these days?" he finally said.

"Luke?" I reached over the counter to retrieve a new bag of mini marshmallows. I was sure Nick had done his homework and knew none of the rest of my family still lived in Bent Creek—just as I was sure he wasn't asking out of some desire to be friendly.

"Yeah. Luke."

I took my time pouring tiny marshmallows into the cute reindeer bowl by the hot chocolate. "He's fine," I said in a neutral voice. If you could call the tension between us, and the fact that he was finally functioning again after losing his wife a little over two years ago, *fine*.

"What's he think of you and my brother?"

My eyebrows shot up, and I crumpled the ends of the marshmallow bag before turning around. Nick was a few feet away, arms still crossed, scowl still fixed to his face. I wanted to tell him Luke's opinion was none of his business, especially since he seemed determined not to like me.

He's Gabe's brother. Even if we might never be friends, I wanted things to be okay between him and Gabe. "Luke's fine with it."

His face remained impassive. "So everything is *fine*."

"Yes." I set the bag of remaining marshmallows on the counter and crossed my arms too. "Why are you so interested in Luke?"

"I figured he might have an opinion on all of this." He paused, his gaze seeming to bore through me. "It's strange that he doesn't, isn't it? Don't you find that strange, Marybeth?"

"To be honest, *Nick*, I don't really care what my brother thinks about who I'm with. It's not any of his business. Or yours." I immediately wished I hadn't said that last part, not when Gabe wanted Nick's help so badly. But he'd gotten under my skin.

Just like he wanted.

He smiled then, but it wasn't friendly. "It is my business when it hurts my family." He paused as I tried to figure out what he meant. "I know what you're doing."

I blinked at him, completely confused. But before I could ask him what he meant, a voice sounded from the doorway.

"Hey. What's this about?" Gabe's frame filled the doorway, and a rush of gratitude swam through me. I wanted to run to him, to curl into his chest while he wrapped his arms around me and assured me that everything was all right.

But all I could imagine was Nick's raised eyebrows and sheer confidence that he was right.

So I held fast to where I was and let Gabe come to me. He wrapped his hand around mine, and it was like lightning shooting up my arm and filling my body with a warmth I'd never known was possible. If there would ever be a day I didn't react to his touch like this, I didn't want to know about it. He pressed his lips against my head, and I turned to smile up at him.

He gave me a tight smile in return. I glanced at Nick, and then back at Gabe. He wanted a moment to deal with his brother, and I was more than happy to give it to him—and to excuse myself from Nick's analytical gaze.

I slid my hand from Gabe's and busied myself behind the counter with a box of Christmas pens that had arrived that morning. Arranging three festive display cups, I sorted the pens as I tried to ignore Gabe and Nick's hushed conversation by the door.

But my eyes kept sliding up toward them. I couldn't hear their whispers over Bing Crosby's crooning from the overhead speakers. Nick stood like a stone, while Gabe leaned in as he spoke quickly.

A few more minutes passed by, and I'd just emptied the box when I heard Nick's voice loud and clear.

"It's not worth saving." He left abruptly, the door hitting the wall as he strode out of the shop.

Gabe stood there for a moment. I set the box down and made my way toward him. I rested a hand on his arm, and he startled.

"Are you all right?" I asked, searching his face for signs of distress. He wanted so badly for Nick to help him figure out how to get the ranch back. He wore the disappointment like a second coat.

"Yeah." He turned and wrapped his arms around my waist. "He's going to change his mind. He wouldn't have gone out to the property if he wasn't thinking about it."

I hoped for Gabe's sake that it would happen. He hadn't said it, but I suspected he had visions of fixing the place up and getting his brothers to visit once in a while. Bringing his family back from the places they'd scattered after Mr. Harker had been sent to prison.

Resting my hands on his chest, I gave him an encouraging smile. "It might take a little time, but I think you're right." My smile faltered a bit as I realized that meant Nick would be sticking around for a while.

"Hey." He crooked his fingers and used them to gently raise my chin. "I set him straight about Luke and you and me."

"Thanks." I sighed as I reached a hand up to take his. "I wish all that stuff would just stay in the past."

"It will, once he wraps his head around it." He looked toward the door where Nick had left. "He felt it a lot more than me. I don't know if it was the last name or that he was closer to Pops or what. But I guess it's not so far-fetched for him to think Luke put you up to . . . whatever Nick thinks he put you up."

"Seducing you with my evil Noble wiles?" I batted my eyelashes at him like some cartoon femme fatale. "So I can steal your . . . truck." It was one of the few things Gabe Creason had to his name after he paid off Durnstorff & Vibert, his former employer, to dissuade their interest in the building that held Bent Creek Christmas.

"The truck is all yours if you stop doing that weird thing with your eyes," he said with a laugh.

"Hey." I punched him gently on the arm. "It's supposed to be sexy."

"I'll show you sexy." And with one fluid motion, he pulled me flush against him and pressed his lips to mine.

I sank into him. A hint of scruff scratched against my skin as my lips opened to him, and my head spun as I held on to him for all I was worth. My brain yelled that a customer could walk in right at that very moment, but I buried that thought with Gabe's warmth and the feel of him pressed against me.

But another thought nagged at the edge of my mind—thanks to Nick—and it was harder to push away.

What if everything that had happened between our families meant it would never work for us?

Chapter Six

Nick

Main Street was too short for the irritation that burned through me. I reached the end where it curved and met the state highway that led up toward the mountain pass and one of the largest ski resorts in this corner of the state.

I turned around, shoving my hands into my pockets, not ready to do battle with cars that couldn't stay on the road and trucks driving thirty miles over. My breath issued white clouds, and I slowed down as I walked back past houses into Bent Creek's small downtown area.

I'd surprised Gabe with the idea that Marybeth might be using him. But as much as I'd hoped that was the case, it was clear I was wrong. I realized it as I watched her answer my questions. And confirmed it with the way she kept looking up at him as he talked to me.

As much as I hated it, she was in love with him.

Gabe felt the same, and *why* these two had to pick each other over everyone else in the world, I'd never get. Had they forgotten the past? Or maybe they didn't care.

The fights. The drugs. The constant push and pull over who was superior. The *gunshots*. I'd never forget it, as long as I lived.

And none of it would've happened if it hadn't been for the Nobles and their greed. They took and took and took, and while Pops wasn't blameless, they were the ones who sent him over the edge.

They were the ones who destroyed our family.

And now Gabe seemed to think they were all fine and good. That they'd changed. Maybe Marybeth was innocent, but her brothers weren't. And it wouldn't be long before Luke or one of the others stopped tolerating it. I knew exactly what Luke was capable of.

Gabe might've brought me here to convince me to help him get the ranch, but I wasn't leaving until I made him see sense about Marybeth.

Main Street opened up into a sickeningly cute array of shops and restaurants—and people.

I didn't notice the people before. I'd avoided Main Street until today, and for good reason. Eyes found me immediately. It was like I'd walked up with a red light flashing over my head.

I'd lived in this town until I was eighteen, and I wasn't naive enough to think word hadn't already made the rounds that I was here. Small towns loved gossip. And another Harker in Bent Creek was probably the best gossip they'd gotten in a while.

I didn't make eye contact with anyone. That would mean stopping and explaining myself, and I didn't plan to be here long enough to bother with that. I looked past them and amused myself with what I imagined they'd say about me. Gabe was the friendly one, the one people had smiled at and asked after. Meanwhile, I was the one who knew too much. The one who looked a little pissed off half the time. The one they assumed had gotten in deep and should've gone to prison right next to Pops.

They were wrong. But no one was rushing up to shake my hand and welcome me back to town.

I passed Marybeth's shop and tried not to think about my brother willingly wrapping his life up in this town again. Moving quickly around a trio of women around my age, I spotted something that piqued my interest across the street.

Mountain Roasters.

I paused half a second before crossing the road. When I pushed the door open, I told myself it was because I could use some coffee.

But I knew that wasn't true the second I laid eyes on Larkin behind the counter. She was whipping up some caffeinated creation for the customer waiting at the register. Her brown eyes darted toward me and widened slightly.

She turned her attention back to the customer, and I shifted from one foot to the other. I didn't know what I'd hoped would happen. That she'd leap over the counter and throw herself into my arms?

That was laughable. And I wasn't sure I wanted it to happen.

I shoved my hands into my pockets as the man in front of me ran his credit card. The stone I'd taken from the driveway that morning sat rough and cold in my right pocket. I wrapped my hand around it, squeezing to force some sense back into my mind where Larkin was concerned.

"Nick," she said. It was a statement, not a question.

The customer was gone, and it was just the two of us. She stood perfectly straight behind the counter, her hands resting on the worn wood. Nails painted a cheerful pink. I smiled at the ghost of a memory. Larkin was one of those girls who always had nice nails. One time I asked her why she took the time for it—after all, I didn't really care if her nails were natural or pink or whatever. She'd smirked at me and told me it wasn't for me. It was for her.

I was glad she still did things that made her happy.

"Hi," I said, lifting my eyes to hers. And I couldn't think of anything else to say. Why did I come in here?

"Coffee?" She pointed at a stack of cups with one pink fingernail.

I nodded, more because it made sense than out of any real desire for a drink.

She poured. The silence around us was deafening. When she set the cup down, I fumbled in my back pocket for my wallet and handed her a few bills.

She gave me some change, and I absentmindedly dropped it into my pocket. The transaction was over. I should have left.

But instead, my fingers grazed that piece of gravel again. On a whim, I pulled it out and set it on the counter.

Larkin looked confused for a second, and then her mouth opened just slightly. She ran her fingers over it, and all I could think of was how badly I wished I was that stupid rock.

"Fool's gold," she said with a little smile.

I returned the smile, pleased beyond reason that I'd made her happy. But I dropped the expression quickly when she retracted her hand.

"It's from the ranch," she said, her eyes still on the gravel.

I nodded. "Yeah. I went out there earlier."

Larkin swallowed, and when she looked up at me again, all I could see was fear.

"I had one of those in my pocket that night . . ."

She didn't need to finish. My heart constricted. I yanked the rock off the counter and dropped it back into my pocket. "I'm sorry. I didn't know."

Larkin shook her head. "How could you?"

It didn't matter. "I should have. I should've paid better attention." I paused, the memory threatening to push its way out and consume me. I pressed it down as I took a deep breath. "That night . . . it never should have happened. You shouldn't have been there."

"Nick." Larkin's voice lowered, and before I knew what was happening, she'd leaned across the counter and wrapped her hand around my wrist. "It wasn't your fault."

The gunfire that erupted that night wasn't. But me putting Larkin in harm's way was. If I was honest with myself, I'd admit it was half the reason I'd left her here in Bent Creek. I didn't trust myself to avoid trouble.

And I didn't know if I'd ever forgive myself for it—any of it.

Chapter Seven

Larkin

IF I CLOSED MY eyes, I could pretend that no time had passed since high school. Since I'd spent evenings cuddled with Nick on his front porch swing.

But I didn't close my eyes, and I didn't dare lose myself in the rosy glow of the past. Not when that past had turned darker than I could've ever imagined back then.

Nick's gray-blue eyes were the color of a lake before a storm. The pain reflected in them was old and well-tried, as if he'd been carrying it around for years and didn't know how to set it down. I squeezed his arm without thinking about it, and a smile faltered on his lips.

He wouldn't let himself smile, not when I'd brought back one of the worst memories of our time together. The sound of gunshots still made me jump. Mr. Harker's shout for us to get down echoed in my mind, and the *thump-thump-thump* of bullets hitting the house and the posts on the front porch was forever seared into my consciousness.

But so was Nick's body pressing mine to the floor of the porch as the sparkling rock I'd picked up earlier dug into my hipbone, his frantic breath in my ear, and the way he clung to me as if I was the only thing that mattered to him that night.

The memories battered my heart, and for a moment, as I looked into Nick's eyes, it seemed we existed in a place no one else could ever enter. No one else would understand me in the way that he did.

Shared trauma did that to a person, I could hear Mom's voice in my head.

And she was right.

I slowly pulled my hand back and clasped my trembling fingers together behind the counter where Nick couldn't see.

Nick cleared his throat. The haunted look disappeared from his eyes as he swept his gaze around the coffee shop.

"How long are you here for?" My voice came out strained, and I reached for the half-empty jug of creamer to give myself something to do.

"As long as it takes." His voice held a serious edge that made me feel a little breathless.

Thankful for a reason to turn away from him, I peeked through the kitchen door to make sure Diego was still sucked into his coloring and the cartoon playing on my phone. Satisfied, I retrieved the creamer from the fridge. When I turned back around, Nick was watching me. I swallowed and forced myself to focus on the jug I needed to refill. "To buy the ranch?"

When he didn't answer, I looked up. He had a pensive look about him, one that suggested he was up to something.

I set the creamer on the counter. "What? I can tell you want to say something."

"I need your help."

My mom had worked in the medical field forever. I knew it was physically impossible for my healthy heart to actually skip a beat, but I swear that was what it did when Nick fixed me with that intense look and asked for my help.

"How is that?" I asked carefully as I returned the creamer to the fridge. I couldn't even imagine what I could do to help him and Gabe find the person who owned the ranch. I didn't have money or connections or anything useful like that.

"Talk to Marybeth. Convince her this thing with her and Gabe is dangerous. She needs to end it."

I blinked at him. He was dead serious. "I . . . Why?" Marybeth was so happy. I couldn't imagine how wrecked she'd be if she and Gabe broke up.

Nick's eyes seemed to bore through me. "You remember what happened to us that night. Do you want to see that happen to Marybeth? Because I sure don't want it happening to my brother. We were lucky. They might not be."

I swallowed as my heart rate ratcheted up. That was the past. Mr. Harker was in prison. Marybeth's dad was in Florida. It was all over, had been for years. "I don't understand. That was a long time ago."

"Was it?"

I hesitated. Then I nodded. "Nothing like that has happened around here since . . ."

"Since Pops went to prison," he finished for me, and I winced at the matter-of-fact way he said it. I remembered the shell of a person he became after the arrest. It was like I barely knew him anymore. Those months before he left were long and painful. But I didn't know then how it felt to be turned inside out by abandonment.

"Yes," I finally said.

"Do you think Noble is going to sit pretty in Florida and let this happen? How long do you think Luke is going to put up with it? And the others—"

"None of her other brothers are still living around here," I said. But it didn't matter. It only took one person to bring back all those old grudges.

"Gabe told me Luke already threatened to shoot him once."

I shook my head. "That was different. He didn't . . ." I trailed off. I couldn't defend that. Luke didn't know then that things were serious between Marybeth and Gabe, but it wasn't like he was their biggest fan now. Marybeth worried about the strain between them. She'd stopped bringing Gabe by their house because it meant days of Luke slamming around the place and glaring at her.

And Luke hadn't exactly been in the best place mentally since he lost his wife in that car wreck. He'd just started to come back to life last fall, taking over the daily operations of the ranch again and relieving some of Marybeth's burden of running two businesses. But he'd still been a shadow of himself, normalcy punctuated with flickers of depression.

Who knew what someone pushed to their very edge might do.

But that didn't mean I was going to meddle in my best friend's relationship.

"Think about it," Nick said, like he knew I'd actually considered it for a second.

"There's nothing to—"

"Mama?"

Diego's voice drew my attention away from Nick's magnetic presence. He stood in the doorway to the kitchen, his big brown eyes going from me to Nick.

"Hey, baby." I scooped him up. It wasn't as easy these days as it used to be. He was growing bigger and taller every day, but I could still perch him on my hip for now. "This is Mr. Nick."

Nick stared at Diego, who gave him a grin in return.

"Hat." Diego pointed at Nick's ever-present cowboy hat. It was such a part of him I barely noticed it.

Nick touched the brim of his hat, as if he'd forgotten it was there too. "Yeah. It's a hat."

I bit my lip to keep from laughing. Diego pushed against me, and I set him down. He immediately toddled around the counter, and pressed himself against Nick's leg.

"Hat." Diego reached his hands up in a request.

"This is Diego," I said to keep myself from laughing at Nick's surprised expression.

He nodded, and then in one swift movement, he squatted down to eye level with Diego. "Well, Diego, you should know I don't let just anyone have my hat. It's really important to me."

Diego gazed up at him, matching Nick's serious look.

"If I let you hold it, will you be careful with it?"

Diego nodded, and Nick was true to his word. He actually handed the hat to Diego.

I cringed, even as the sweet gesture melted some corner of my heart. "He's not exactly the most gentle—"

Diego immediately pressed his hand into it, making a dent.

Nick stood, grinning. Which wasn't what I'd expected at all. "Nah, he didn't hurt it. It'll come out."

Still, I'd feel better if that hat was back where it was supposed to be and out of the hands of my eager two-year-old. "Diego, can you hand it back to Mr. Nick?"

"Just Nick is fine." Nick held out his hand as Diego obediently returned the hat.

"Mr. Nick," Diego repeated. And then he immediately wrapped his arms around Nick's leg.

I covered my mouth to keep from laughing as Nick's eyebrows disappeared into his hair.

"It's a compliment," I said once I recovered. "Diego's an excellent judge of character. Well, most of the time. He called your brother 'Mean Man' for a while."

Nick laughed. "Remind me to rub that in next time I see Gabe."

"Hey, Diego." I pulled a Hershey's kiss from my apron pocket, a bribe I kept on hand for moments like this. He spotted it and let go of Nick's leg to run behind the counter. "Why don't you color for a little longer? Gramma's going to be here soon to get you."

He nodded and ran into the back room. "He's not supposed to be here. If Charlie finds out I've got him behind the door during my shift, he'll fire me for good this time." I tried to press down the anxiety that arose with that thought.

"Charlie Gates? He won't hear it from me." Nick had returned the hat to his head. His eyes were more blue than gray now, and I had the sudden urge to ask him to give me that rock back. He held my gaze a moment, and his brow furrowed. "You serious about Gates? I remember that little—" He paused, catching himself as if whatever adjective he was going to use to describe Charlie would offend me. "You want me to talk to him?"

My eyes widened. The last thing I needed was Nick tracking down Charlie Gates and acting the role of the angry boyfriend. He'd fire me for sure then. "No. Definitely not."

Nick shrugged. "Let me know if you change your mind."

I wouldn't, but I wanted to hug him for offering, as misplaced as the gesture was. I guess I'd forgotten how protective Nick could be.

But he wasn't my boyfriend. He had no reason to protect me . . . unless he felt guilty for what he'd done. Or maybe . . .

No, I couldn't even let my mind go there. But I still found myself watching the way his fingers curled around the coffee cup. When my eyes wandered back up to his, I remembered all those times he'd caught me staring at him when we were teenagers. He used to tease me about it, but the truth was, he was hard to look away from.

"I'll think about it," I found myself saying. "About Marybeth."

He nodded. "See you soon, Larkin." With a tug at his hat, he was gone.

The sound of my name on his lips rumbled through my mind as deeply as his voice, and I stared at the door until it opened again.

Mom stopped just inside the door. One look at me and she started shaking her head.

There was no way she missed Nick leaving the coffee shop. "He bought coffee. That's all."

"Are you sure?" She pushed a length of hair from her eyes. "Because your face says something different."

"I'm sure." I turned abruptly to get Diego.

Pausing just inside the door to the kitchen, I swallowed and straightened my shoulders. I *was* sure.

There was no way I'd fall for Nick Harker again.

Chapter Eight

Nick

The Dowling Bed and Breakfast was as frilly and old-fashioned as I remembered it.

I parked my truck next to Gabe's in the narrow set of spaces along the street and wondered again why he was staying here. There were plenty of places up by the interstate, like the Slope Motel. Cheaper and more anonymous. No one you knew asking questions.

I shut the truck door and wished we'd met outside of town again, like we had since I got here. Maybe this was part of Gabe's insidious plan to convince me that I actually *wanted* to help him get the ranch back—or worse, convince me that I missed this place.

I climbed the steps to the old Victorian, flexed my hands, and took a deep breath. Then I opened the door and waited for the interrogation. *Nick Harker, is that you? Where have you been? What are you doing these days? How are your brothers?* And then, if they were especially nosy, there would be a hushed, *Did you hear about Gabe and Mary-beth Noble?*

Those had been the questions I'd dodged from the brave souls who actually talked to me the couple of times I'd ventured into town. Which I'd only done twice so far, first to see Larkin and then to meet up with Kyle Clemmons, a football teammate turned real estate agent who'd been helping Gabe off and on with learning more about the ranch and its current owner. But most people said nothing. They just stared and whispered into their phones.

And I really didn't want to know what they were saying.

"Nick!"

I recognized the voice immediately as I blinked against the dim entryway of the B&B. "Hey, Suzanne." Suzanne Dowling had been a cheerleader when Gabe and I were on the football team. She'd been the life of the party, the girl that half the guys wished they could have. But more than her looks, I remembered her as simply . . . nice.

"I was wondering when you'd come by." She shifted the baby she was holding to her other arm. She actually seemed genuinely happy to see me.

I nodded at the baby. "Is that your little one?"

Her smile lit up the room. "Yes. This is Annie." She turned the baby just slightly so I could see her.

Tiny, perfect features looked back at me. Annie blinked, and some piece of my heart that I didn't know existed melted just a little. "She's beautiful."

"Thank you." Suzanne beamed and tucked Annie against her shoulder again. "Are you here to see Gabe?"

"Yeah. Is he . . .?" I gestured toward the stairs, which were more than just stairs. They were wide and winding with graceful polished balusters that meandered with old-style grace and elegance up to the second floor instead of simply doing the job of taking you there.

"Room five. At the top of the stairs." She adjusted Annie's blanket before fixing her gaze back on me. "Do you need a room too? We have a few available."

Judging from the mostly empty parking, they had more than a few. But as nice as Suzanne was, I had no interest in staying somewhere like this, with people I knew seeing every movement I made. I'd keep the anonymity of the Slope Motel. "I'm fine," I said. "Thanks. It's good to see you, Suzanne."

"Same," she said with a broad grin that brought a pang to my heart.

I turned away quickly and made for the stairs. Bent Creek was trying its damnedest to get to me, but I wouldn't let it. For every one of those good memories, a bad one was waiting around the corner.

This town ruined my family, I reminded myself. And the only reason I was here was to get Gabe out before he let it happen to him all over again.

He opened the door before I could knock. "Thought I heard your voice downstairs."

When I raised my eyebrows because of the sheer distance between this room and the foyer, he shrugged. "Old houses. You can hear everything."

I shut the door behind me, now even more more glad I kept my room by the interstate. "How long are you planning to stay here? This place can't be cheap." I looked around at the half-made bed with the ruffled comforter, the lacy knitted-looking things on the dresser, and the fussy paintings hanging on the wall. Even the window had some kind of design etched into the top half of the glass.

"It's not bad," Gabe said vaguely. "I like it. It's nice to see friendly faces."

I shuddered inwardly at that as I sat in an overstuffed armchair by the window. Suzanne was fine, but I couldn't imagine everyone fixing stares on me every time I came or went.

"Besides, I'm thinking of asking Marybeth if she wants to get an apartment this summer." Gabe leaned against the wall like what he said was no big deal.

I wrenched my jaw shut from where it had fallen open. "You're going to do what?"

"You heard me." Gabe didn't miss a beat. "I need something more permanent, and she needs to get out of that ranch house. And it's the logical next step for us."

I swallowed the first thing I wanted to say. *You're going to tie yourself to a Noble in a lease?* "Do you think that's smart?"

His face turned stony. "I don't need your opinion on my relationship. I thought I made that clear."

It sounded like he *did* need my opinion, no matter what he'd said back in Marybeth's shop, but I had to tread carefully. "I was talking to Larkin earlier."

"Oh?" Gabe sounded oddly hopeful, and I felt a little bad about puncturing that balloon.

"She brought up that night at the ranch."

Gabe's jaw twitched. He knew which night I meant. There had been other incidents, some involving gunfire, some not, but never anything at our home. Never anything so malicious. He hadn't been home, but it wasn't anything he'd forget easily. "That was a long time ago."

"It could happen again." I sat back in the chair, waiting for it to sink in for him.

Gabe pressed away from the wall, pacing across the room before turning to face me. And by the look on his face, I could tell he was ready for a fight. "You think Luke Noble—the man who can barely keep his ranch going because he's still grieving for his wife—is going to roll up to whatever place Marybeth and I find and start shooting?"

I forced myself not to cringe. When he said it, it sounded ridiculous. But he didn't know the truth. I'd never told him, because I hadn't ever thought it was necessary. Now I almost wished I had.

I danced around it for now. "Grief does strange things to people. Didn't he already meet you with a rifle?"

He brushed it off with a shake of his head. "There's nothing Luke Noble can throw at me that I can't handle. Now what's this about Larkin? You hanging out with her again?"

I looked toward the window. A woman with blonde hair was carrying an armload of books across the street. I squinted. It was Emily Foley. Were we the only people who'd actually left this town?

I glanced back at Gabe, who was waiting for an answer. I should've known he'd ask the second Larkin's name left my lips. "Not really. She threw a coffee at me the other day." Okay, maybe that wasn't fair to her, but I'd say anything to get Gabe off my back.

Gabe smirked. "And that made you see her again." It was a statement, not a question, because he knew. Whether it was from my reaction or from town gossip or from Marybeth, he *knew*.

"It's nothing. I'm just being nice after . . . Well, you know." Which sounded like pity, even though it was anything but that.

"Good. Although I should warn you that Marybeth will personally run you back to Texas if you break Larkin's heart again."

"Oh, for God's sake, I'm not going to *break her heart*. I'm just . . ." What? What *was* I doing?

"Being nice?" Gabe filled in for me, that smirk back on his face.

"Yeah." I sat up, ready to have that conversation over. "How are you paying for this place, by the way? Did you get a job? Marybeth Noble isn't going to move in with an unemployed slacker who's obsessed with a piece of land."

Gabe looked pissed for a half a second before laughing. It was a good sound, one that brought back all those times we used to ride each other for stupid stuff when we were teenagers. "Kind of. I've been doing some odd jobs on some ranches around town. And I'm not completely broke."

That was news to me. Last he told me, he'd given his savings to get his old firm off Marybeth's back.

"All right, *mostly* not broke. But nothing you need to worry about. I'd be staying in that dump by the highway with you if I was in that bad of a shape."

It was my turn to laugh, and I realized I'd *missed* my brother. No one ever got me the way he did. I'd gotten along fine with the guys I worked with at the ranch in Texas, but there had never been anyone like Gabe.

"Did Kyle catch you in town?" Gabe asked as I stood up.

"Not since yesterday."

"He texted me earlier. Another ranch outside of town sold a few weeks ago. He found out who the buyer was."

I half expected him to say Luke Noble, even though it seemed Luke wasn't in any mental shape to be buying up property.

"Chestnut Moon, LLC," Gabe filled in for me.

"Really." Against my better judgment, I was intrigued.

"Yeah."

I shouldn't care. I shouldn't be even remotely interested, but when the same untraceable company that bought up our ranch also bought another one . . .

I wanted to know who it was.

Chapter Nine

Marybeth

"Sucker?" Diego thrusted a bright pink candy on a stick at me the second I opened the door.

"I think that one's all yours, buddy," I said with a laugh. He nodded seriously as Larkin ushered him through the open door.

"Thank you for watching him." Larkin dropped a bag that I knew would be filled with toys and snacks onto one of the armchairs in the living room. "Especially on a Monday." She made a face like she thought she was putting me out on the one day of the week my shop was closed.

"It's okay. I canceled the plans Gabe and I had to go to Bali this morning."

She smiled, but it didn't make her laugh the way I hoped it would. "What's wrong?" I asked.

"Nothing's wrong, really." Larkin tossed the words over her shoulder as she rescued the bag from Diego's fingers. "You need a snack?" she asked him.

When he nodded, she pulled out a bag of crackers and a foil-covered plate, and led him into the kitchen. I grabbed a paper towel as she got Diego settled on a stack of pillows at the table.

"For you," she said, handing me the plate.

I pulled back the foil to find a stack of fudgy brownies. "I'm going to have to hide these or Luke will eat them all. Now sit and tell me." I pointed to the small breakfast bar that flanked the opening to the living room.

Larkin perched on one of the chairs—the same one she'd chosen every time she'd come over here since we were twelve and realized we were best friends. I set the plate down and sat too, waiting for her to say something.

She pushed a piece of her long dark hair back behind her ear and glanced at Diego, who was happily munching on crackers as he watched an episode of *Bluey* on Larkin's old phone.

"I'm worried," she finally said. "About you and Gabe."

I didn't expect *that*. Especially considering how happy Larkin seemed to be that we'd gotten together over Christmas. "What do you mean?"

She ran a painted fingernail over a tiny divot in the wooden bar. "It's . . . Well, you remember what happened with Nick? Back in high school?"

I thought for a second, but I couldn't figure out what she meant. "A lot of things happened with Nick," I reminded her.

Larkin clasped her hands in her lap. "Fall, sophomore year. When I was over at Nick's and . . ." She trailed off as pain glimmered in her eyes.

And I knew exactly what she was talking about. That one awful night, where someone drove up the Harkers' driveway and fired shots at Larkin, Nick, Mr. Harker, and Nick and Gabe's younger brother

Jackson. The worst injury had been a graze along Mr. Harker's arm. And when Mr. Harker blamed Dad, it was the beginning of the end for Gabe and Nick's family.

And ours too, if I was being honest.

"That was an awful time." The threats against us from Mr. Harker were terrifying, but I knew it was nothing compared to what Larkin had experienced.

She reached out and took my hand. "Please, Marybeth, I don't want it to happen again. To you."

I tilted my head, letting the past fade back to where it belonged. "It won't. That wasn't my family, remember? And it was a long time ago."

"But how do you know?" Her eyes were wide, as if the unknown shooters from that night lurked right around the corner of our house, just waiting for the right moment.

"Larkin." I squeezed her hand. "I believe my dad. He wouldn't ever do something like that. Mr. Harker was always just looking for a reason to rile things up between them. Besides, years have passed. Nick's dad is in prison. All that stuff is over with."

Larkin didn't say anything, so I continued. "Whoever that was, they're gone. And they have no reason to come back. Gabe and I are fine."

She pressed her lips together before looking away.

I watched her quietly for a moment. Larkin hadn't spoken of that night in years. She hadn't even visited a therapist about it since before Diego was born. So, why bring it up now?

There was only one answer.

"Is this because Nick is back in town?" I asked gently.

She sighed before slowly looking back at me. "I'm sorry. I'm just . . . so confused. Seeing Nick is bringing back so many memories. And then he brought . . . Well, we ended up talking about that night. And he's afraid too, but Gabe won't listen to him, so he asked me if I'd talk to you."

My eyebrows flew up to my hairline. Nick was behind this. I should've known.

"I want you to be happy, and I think you and Gabe are so good for each other, but Nick isn't wrong. I didn't bring it up because he asked me to. I did it because once I started to think about it, I felt afraid for you. And Marybeth, I can't imagine anything bad happening to you. But now I'm just so confused." Her eyes had a frantic, haunted look, and I knew without a doubt that Larkin was telling the truth.

But that didn't mean I couldn't be annoyed at Nick for bringing it up in the first place. He was working extra hard to drive a wedge between Gabe and me.

I stood and reached over to hug my friend. "Thank you for looking out for me." I stepped back, keeping my hands on her shoulders. "But trust me when I say everything is okay. All of that stuff is in the past. Gabe and I are just two regular people in a relationship, that's all."

She nodded as the side door opened. Luke tromped in, dropping snow and mud across the kitchen floor. He rumpled Diego's hair as I cringed at the mess he left.

"Hey, Diego."

Diego grinned up at him with a mouth full of crackers, and my heart cracked as Luke gave him a sad smile. He and Liz had talked about having kids, and seeing the way he looked at Diego, who was sitting at our kitchen table . . . I wondered if it made him think of what he'd never have with Liz.

"Larkin." Luke nodded at my friend, who slid off the barstool. There was an undertone to his voice, one I recognized far too well, especially since I'd started seeing Gabe. I knew exactly what was coming.

I stepped forward to interrupt, brownie plate in hand, but it was too late.

"Nick Harker's back, I hear."

It wasn't a question, but Larkin nodded anyway. She held up a hand. "I know what you're going to say. Mom and Marybeth have already said it—even Mrs. Foley said something the other day." Her forehead wrinkled slightly, and I tried to imagine what the older woman who frequented my shop for holiday-themed baking supplies might have told Larkin about Nick.

I wanted to tell her that she didn't need to explain herself to my brother, of all people, even if I agreed with him. "Larkin—"

Her phone chimed, cutting me off. She pulled it from her purse and stared at it for a moment before clenching her fingers tighter around it.

"All I wanted was to warn you to be careful," Luke said, crossing his arms and leaning back against the countertop.

I watched him a moment as he worked his jaw, clearly trying hard not to say anything else. He held back with Larkin. He saw her as a little sister, but he wouldn't dare try to order her around, as he did with me.

Not that it had worked.

"I have to go." Larkin's voice was distracted as she clutched the phone in her hand and moved fast toward the living room. "Bye, Diego baby. Thanks, Marybeth."

And before I could say anything, she'd swept through the door.

When I glanced back at Diego, I found my brother watching him with a wistful expression, and my heart broke all over again. I'd carried Luke for so long. Hiring and firing ranch hands when he couldn't get out of bed. Feeding the horses while he sat in front of the TV without really seeing it. Making sure he survived his own grief.

If I had to do that again with Larkin, I might collapse under the weight of it all.

Chapter Ten

Larkin

I chewed on the inside of my cheek as I looked at the text again. *Creepy* didn't even begin to describe it.

I saw you with him.

A shiver made my arms break out in goosebumps despite the warmth inside Mountain Roasters. I set my phone down to get a large chai for Kyle Clemmons, the real estate agent who had an office nearby. But the second Kyle left, I opened up the text again.

I didn't recognize the number. When I googled it, all I got back was a bunch of gibberish on sites I didn't dare click on. The only thing I could figure out was that the area code came from Seattle.

I didn't know anyone from Seattle.

Maybe they'd sent the text to the wrong number. I twisted the corner of my apron as I realized exactly how unlikely that was. If I didn't have the number in my contacts, the texter probably didn't have me in his (or hers?) either. Which meant they had to type out my number to send me a text. And while I guess it was possible they could have reversed a number or whatever to send their stalker-y message to someone else who also wasn't in their contact list, it seemed like a really slim possibility.

Especially since I knew exactly who "him" would be.

The chime over the door rang, and I startled, half-expecting to see the creepy texter. Instead, it was a couple holding hands and looking ready to hit the slopes in matching gear. As the woman scanned the menu, Flannery Jacobs arrived with her baby in a stroller. I patiently answered the first woman's questions as a few more people arrived.

Mountain Roasters had gone from empty to slammed in a matter of five minutes.

I worked as fast as I could, finally filling the first couple's order. I turned to grab a lid and nearly ran right into Charlie—my boss.

"Larkin, what is this? How long have these people been waiting?" He gestured at the line with one skinny arm as the pencil-thin mustache he'd grown twitched.

"Not very long. They all arrived at once," I said, a little short of breath as I reached around him for the lid I needed.

"You can't make people wait this long! It's bad for business."

I turned away and fought the urge to roll my eyes. The only thing bad for business was the fact we were in Bent Creek, Population 3, but I wasn't about to say that to my boss. Sometimes I wasn't sure how this place stayed open, but I was glad it did.

I needed the job.

"And what is this? I told you not to bring your . . . your creations in here. We can't sell these!" He pointed at the plastic container that held a couple of the fudge brownies I'd also given to Marybeth.

"They're for me." They weren't. They were for Mrs. Foley, who gave me really good feedback on my baking, but I wasn't about to share that with Charlie.

He shook his head. "No personal food up front. The health department will slap us with a fine, and then what can I do?" He paused to take a breath, and just as I was turning back to the customers, he added, "Come on, Larkin. People are waiting!"

I gritted my teeth to keep the words I wanted to say inside. Charlie was getting louder. Flannery pushed her stroller back and forth and peeked around the man in front of her. Warmth colored my cheeks, but I forced a smile at the indecisive couple as I turned the credit card reader toward them.

"Thank you for coming to Mountain Roasters!" My voice was high-pitched and overly sweet. "What can I get for you today?" I asked Flannery.

Her eyes darted to Charlie, who I realized was hovering right over my shoulder, his eyes glued to my phone. "Were you texting? Is that why there's such a line?"

I dug my fingers into my palms as poor Flannery looked from me to Charlie. "No. There's a line because the shop is busy." I kept my voice even, which wasn't exactly easy. But I *needed* this job.

"Really? Because your phone says otherwise." Charlie held up my phone, which showed a grayed-out text notification over a picture of Diego.

My heart slammed against my ribcage. It couldn't be the anonymous texter again. It was probably just Marybeth, sending me some cute story about Diego or asking if he could have something sweet.

"Larkin. We've had this conversation before." His voice was louder, irritated—and embarrassing.

My face grew hotter, but he kept going, oblivious to the other people around us. Flannery started to back up, slowly rolling the stroller backward.

"I appreciate that you're a mom, but you can worry about your kid outside of work hours. If you can't concentrate on work when you're at work, then we're going to have a problem."

"Hey, Larkin." I whipped my eyes from Charlie to the voice that seemed to have come out of nowhere.

Nick leaned an arm on the counter, taking up the space Flannery vacated but that the next people in line hadn't filled. "Charlie Gates," he said in an even tone.

My breath caught. All I could think about was Nick's offer to *speak to* Charlie on my behalf. I shook my head just slightly at him. *Please don't . . .*

But Nick wasn't looking at me. I glanced at Charlie, whose rat-like face seemed to pinch before he gave Nick a shallow smile. "Good to see you, Nick. Larkin and I were talking. Can you give us—"

"I didn't hear talking, Gates." Nick's voice was a quiet roar, the anger boiling under the surface. I didn't know how Charlie didn't hear it. But he kept looking at Nick with that fake smile.

"Nick," I said, willing him to look at me and *not* cause a scene right here where I worked.

But his eyes were fixed on Charlie.

Charlie gave a little laugh. "We're just wrapping up our conversation, and then Larkin can get your coffee."

"I don't want coffee. And that wasn't a conversation. All I heard was you berating a woman for worrying about her child." Nick's eyes were steel, and Charlie finally seemed to notice. His smile fell away, and he turned to face Nick.

I swallowed hard. "Nick, don't," I forced myself to say, even though I knew it was pointless. The facts of the situation didn't even matter at this point. Nick was on a mission, and I didn't know how to stop him. It was the thing I'd always both admired and feared about him.

He straightened and pressed both hands against the top of the counter, his gaze never leaving Charlie's face. "If you're going to fire her, be a man and *do* it. Because I swear, if I hear about you making her miserable again because she has a kid, I'll come find you. And you won't like what happens next."

The entire shop was silent except for the slow dripping of the coffee machine behind me. Charlie's face went bright red, and I couldn't decide if I wanted to crawl under a table or throw my arms around Nick.

Charlie blinked a few times, turned to me with a curt "Get to work," and then banged through the door to the kitchen.

Nick's gaze went to me, and the steel softened into a cloudy blue. "Are you all right?"

"I . . . I don't know," I said honestly.

Nick nodded, as if that was a perfectly acceptable answer. He disappeared behind the line, and when I finally gathered myself enough to take the next customer's order, I spotted him sitting at a table in the corner. Like my own personal bodyguard.

I didn't need him. I was perfectly capable of taking care of myself. After all, I'd done it for years. And I certainly didn't need the guy who'd stomped all over my heart when I was sixteen swooping in and saving the day now. I should have been mad at him.

And I was—a little. Just thinking of how embarrassed I'd felt was enough to churn up every feeling of righteous indignation I could muster.

Yet I still found myself glancing toward that corner. At Nick, sprawled out on that chair as if he owned the place. And wondering why, after all these years, he still made my heart trip over itself.

Chapter Eleven

Nick

I'd stayed at the coffee shop until Charlie Gates went slinking out the front door. Satisfied that he'd leave Larkin alone for at least the rest of the day, I'd left her to her coffee and customers.

But curiosity—and a need to know that Gates wouldn't take out his embarrassment on Larkin—had me standing outside Mountain Roasters first thing the next morning.

The town was quiet this early, shops and restaurants closed up. The only spot that showed any life was the pancake place at the other end of Main Street. I sucked in the cold air as I adjusted the strap from the laptop bag over my shoulder. I didn't usually mind the quiet, at least not in Texas. But here . . . it stirred up too many memories. Walking hand-in-hand with Larkin after the Holiday Hope dance. Visiting the candy shop with Gabe's mom and my brothers. Pops teaching me to parallel park along the street. And the slow, dawning realization that everyone in town saw us differently.

It hadn't happened fast. It took years. But after every incident, people pulled away a little more. Until at the end, no one lifted their hand to wave, their eyes quickly found something else to look at, and whispers followed me wherever I went.

It was hard to reconcile the friendly Bent Creek of my childhood with what it had become when I'd left. And I didn't know that I even *wanted* to.

Could you forgive a place when it had no heart to forgive you?

"Nick?"

I jerked my head toward Larkin's voice. Peeling myself off the outside of the building, I flashed her a grin. "Mornin', beautiful."

I cringed inside as she raised her eyebrows. I hadn't planned on saying that. But old habits died hard, and I sure wasn't lying when I said it. Her brown eyes sparkled in the morning sun, and her cheeks were pink with cold under the hood of her coat.

"Hi, Mr. Nick."

I was so focused on Larkin that I hadn't even noticed her sidekick. Diego rounded his mother's leg and smiled up at me.

"Hey, big guy," I said back to him.

"What are you doing here?" Larkin had fished a set of keys from her pocket and was fitting one of them into the lock on the door.

"Getting coffee."

She gave me a sidelong glance, and I shrugged.

"I brought a laptop." I lifted my shoulder where the battered old machine sat inside the bag. "Thought I'd do some work."

"Hmm." She pressed the door open and dropped the keys into her pocket. "I thought you were a ranch hand."

It was my turn to raise my eyebrows, because I was pretty sure she hadn't asked what I'd been doing with my life. Which meant she either went out of her way to ask Marybeth, who probably knew from Gabe, or she simply knew me too well to think I'd be doing anything else.

"I'm doing some work for Gabe," I amended. Like tracking down more information on this Chestnut Moon company. Despite the fact I had no intention of putting any money behind this venture of Gabe's, he'd gotten me curious.

"Oh, really?" Larkin led the way inside. Diego climbed up into a chair and began rearranging the napkin holder on the table.

I followed and dropped the laptop on the corner table. "He's my brother and my best friend. Why wouldn't I help him out?" I paused. "At least a little."

"Well, do me a favor, okay?" Larkin pushed back her hood, letting the waves of dark hair spill out. I wanted so badly to run my fingers through it that I had to clench my hand to my side.

"What's that?" I managed to say.

"If Charlie comes back, don't get up in his face again? I can handle myself."

I narrowed my eyes a little. Was she serious? "I won't stand by while a snake like Gates belittles a woman."

Larkin watched me a moment. "Any woman?" Her voice was quiet.

"Yes." Which was true, but she didn't know the extent of what I'd felt when I saw what that man was doing. The thoughts that had crossed my mind, and none of them ended with him in any shape to walk.

Only Larkin could make me want to put everything on the line like that. I hadn't remembered that until yesterday.

Larkin's dark eyes watched me for half a beat more, but it felt as if time had stopped.

Then, abruptly, she turned and held out a hand to Diego, who slid off the chair and let her unbutton his coat. "Now, remember what I said?"

"No noise. Be invisible," he recited, tripping over the last word.

"Invisible. Right. Let's get you set up in back." She tossed his coat over her arm and took his hand.

"Is he staying here with you all day?" I asked, curiosity getting the best of me.

"No, just a few hours. Marybeth will stop by and take him to her shop when it opens." Larkin spoke lightly, like it wasn't a big deal, but the way she chewed her lip afterward said something different.

"Gates won't be okay with that," I said, more to myself than to her, but she nodded.

"My mom's sick. She picked up something at the hospital, and she can't keep up with him today. So this is all I've got." She gazed down at Diego, and I didn't have to be close to feel the fierce love she had for that little boy.

He was lucky, and I hoped he knew that. To have a mom here and ready to do anything to take care of him. I had that twice—once with my own mom, and once with Katrina, Gabe's mother. And both for way too short a time.

Larkin had a worried look in her eye as she ran a hand over Diego's hair. If Charlie Gates showed up while Diego was here . . . Fire lit up my insides at the thought of dealing with him again. It wouldn't be pretty. And as much as I couldn't stand the guy, Larkin clearly needed this job. Which meant Diego needed to not be here.

Just at that moment, he looked up at me with big brown eyes—an exact replica of his mother's. He grinned, and some cemented-over corner of my heart cracked.

"I'll watch him." The words were out of my mouth before the thought had finished crossing my mind.

Larkin's eyes widened slightly. "No, you don't have to do that."

Any doubt I had vanished. All those years of dealing with my little brothers were about to pay off. "I might not look like it, but I'm good with kids."

"I know that," she said quickly. "It's just . . . I mean, I trust you and all, but Diego can be a handful."

"I can handle it." I flashed Diego a grin, and he jumped up and down.

"I want to go with Mr. Nick!" he said in that cute, high-pitched kid voice.

I squatted down to his eye level. "We can check out the park."

"It's covered in snow," Larkin said.

"So? It's more fun that way. And when we get cold, we'll go to the library."

"The library?" Larkin lifted her eyebrows.

I stood up. "Yes, I've been there before."

She rolled her eyes. "That's not what I meant. Maybe." Her mouth quirked up into a half smile.

I threw a hand over my heart and looked down at Diego. "Your mama thinks I'm a dumb cowboy who can't read."

"Nick! Seriously." Larkin swatted my arm, but she was smiling. "I just don't want to take advantage of you."

"You're not. I promise, or I wouldn't have offered. You can pay me in cookies." My mouth watered at the thought of the peanut butter chocolate-chip cookies she used to make.

She drew her lip between her teeth and looked from me to Diego, who was dancing with excitement. "All right. Fine. You only have to keep him for a few hours, then bring him back here to meet Marybeth."

I felt like I'd won a victory in the war to get Larkin to forgive me. I held up a hand toward Diego, and he gave me five immediately. "Let's go, little man. Get your coat."

Larkin helped Diego put his coat and mittens on. He held out his hand, and I took it, cradling those tiny fingers in mine. It felt awkward, and yet at the same time, it set off some primal urge to fight off anyone who might ever cause this kid to hurt.

Larkin's gaze softened as she looked at us. The crack in my heart widened.

"We'll be back soon. Don't forget about those cookies."

"I forgot that recipe," she said with a grin.

"Impossible." I shouldered my laptop bag and led Diego out the door, not sure exactly what I'd gotten myself into, but knowing I'd throw myself into it over and over to have Larkin look at me that way again.

Chapter Twelve

Larkin

If nothing could have prepared me for Nick offering to watch Diego, I definitely never could have expected to see them burst back through the door of Mountain Roasters, Diego giggling like crazy while Nick chased him with his hands held up like giant claws.

"Mama! Mama! Monster!" Diego ran laughing around the counter and threw himself against my legs.

The coffee shop was empty for the moment, the morning rush over. Which meant I could grab hold of Diego and prop him up on my hip, far away from the "monster" on the other side of the counter. "You're safe now. Except maybe for . . . the tickle monster!" I tickled Diego's side, and he threw himself into another laughing fit.

Nick laughed too, his hands now resting on the counter.

"Run!" Diego shouted, and I set him down. He raced into the kitchen, where I imagined he was hiding from the tickle monster.

"How was he?" I asked, turning toward Nick.

"Great. That kid is a lot of fun." Nick's usual somber expression had softened into something more contented—and tired.

"He's also got a lot of energy," I said with a little smile.

"You can say that again." He pulled off his hat and ran a hand through that dark hair. And when he looked at me, all I could think of was how I used to thread my own hands through his hair when we kissed.

My face flamed with the memory, and I glanced down at the counter and pretended to pick at a nonexistent speck of dirt. "Thank you," I said, not daring to look up yet.

"Any time."

Did he mean that? Or was he just being nice? I went to the kitchen door, buying myself a moment while I checked on Diego. He'd settled himself just inside with a coloring book and crayons. I shut the door and went back to the counter, where I finally looked up at Nick, a lock of hair falling into my face. He still wore that contented expression, but his eyes darkened some when he caught my gaze.

He meant it.

I could tell without him saying a word, but he spoke anyway. "It made me think . . ." He trailed off, not finishing what I so desperately wanted to find out.

But instead of saying anything else, he reached down and brushed my hair from my face. My breath caught as my skin prickled in the wake of his touch. His thumb lingered on the side of my cheek, and I thought I might melt under the heat of it right where I stood.

This was wrong. The words echoed faintly in some faraway corner of my mind. Somewhere that remembered what Nick had done. But that seemed like so long ago, and now was now. He was here.

And he was more than I ever expected him to be.

"Larkin." His voice sounded strangled, as if he was fighting off just as many emotions as I was.

My mind flitted between pulling away and throwing myself over the counter to kiss him. But a chime from the door whisked my indecisiveness away.

I jumped backward as Nick turned, his hand falling away.

"Hello." Marybeth stood uncertainly by the door. "I came to get Diego?"

"Um, yeah." I wiped my suddenly damp hands across my apron and crossed to the kitchen door. "Diego! Marybeth is here. Can you put the crayons back in the box for me?"

He nodded and immediately started dropping crayons into their plastic box. He was such a good kid, and I couldn't keep the smile from my face as I watched him.

"He'll be out in a sec," I said to Marybeth.

She'd moved to the counter, next to Nick, who was turning his hat around in his hands. "I should go." He gathered his laptop bag from the floor and replaced his hat. He nodded at Marybeth, and his gaze lingered on me for a moment before he left.

"I interrupted something," Marybeth said the second the door closed behind him.

I groaned, closing my eyes. I didn't know how I felt about whatever it was that had just passed between me and Nick.

"Something good . . . or not?" Marybeth said carefully.

"I don't know." I shrugged as Diego pushed open the door behind me. "It's confusing."

"Marybet!" Diego exclaimed when he spotted Marybeth. He'd graduated recently from calling her *Maybet*.

"Hi, Diego!" She gave him a hug when he came around the counter. Looking up at me, she said, "You know, I'm going to be heartbroken when he finds that last *h*."

"Me too," I said.

"Are you ready to go to my shop?" she asked Diego.

He nodded. He was still wearing his coat from earlier.

"I need help sorting some ornaments today. Can you do that?"

He nodded again.

"Put your mittens on before you go," I said to him. He fished them from his coat pockets, and Marybeth bent to help him.

When she straightened, she took his hand and turned to me. "As much as Nick is annoying me with his agenda against Gabe and me, you know I support you no matter what. I don't want to see you hurt, but if you think he's changed, then . . ."

"Thank you." I couldn't ask for a better friend than Marybeth. It meant the world to me that she had my back in anything.

Diego waved to me as he left with her, and I leaned against the counter, resting my chin in my hand.

It was all so confusing. Were my feelings real or were they remnants of what Nick and I used to have? I trusted him with Diego, but could I trust him with my heart? Could I even take that chance again?

What did I want?

What did *he* want?

I closed my eyes, and it was like I could feel his hand on my face again, gentle and warm. It was so familiar that it felt as if we'd never been apart, and yet it was terrifying at the same time.

I had Diego. I couldn't just go falling for my old boyfriend. Diego was old enough now that any relationship I had would be one he remembered, for good or for bad. I couldn't let myself do anything that could hurt him.

I sighed, unable to find any answers but letting my mind wander again, back to the way Nick had looked at me. Back to what he'd been about to say before he'd cut himself off.

My phone buzzed in my pocket. For a second, I hoped it was Nick, until I remembered he didn't have my number. It was probably Mom, asking me to pick up some chicken noodle soup on my way home.

I pulled out my phone and unlocked it. And then I wished I hadn't.

You're a terrible mother.

I sucked in a breath. Another text came immediately.

You trusted a drug dealer with Diego.

Chapter Thirteen

Marybeth

"Noel, quit! That's enough. Let Carol have some." I scolded the chickens like they were children. Not that they understood what I was saying.

It was a weirdly warm day—the kind that reminded me it wouldn't be long until spring—and my boots sunk into the mud where the snow had melted. Gabe was coming to pick me up soon, and I had to get the chickens fed first.

Well, *I* didn't have to. Luke would've done it, which was a nice change after being in charge of everything on this ranch for so long. But honestly, I really liked the chickens. I always had.

"Hey, Holly." I backed up to let one of the Rhode Island Reds get to the feed.

"You really are obsessed with Christmas." Larkin's voice sounded from behind me.

"And chickens," I confessed as I exited the enclosure. I shut the gate securely behind me. I'd learned the hard way as a kid that there were far too many wild animals that liked chickens. "What are you doing here?"

She pulled her face into that same pinched look she'd met me with yesterday when she came to get Diego at my shop. I'd figured then that she was just trying to work out whatever it was she had going on with Nick, so I didn't pry. But maybe she did want to talk about it.

"Is it Nick?" I asked gently. I wanted to be there for her no matter what, but if she were to drag out my honest opinion, it was that she was much better off without him around. While Gabe had mostly stayed out of his stepfather's business in high school, everyone knew that Nick had been involved, at least for a little while. Long enough to make a reputation for himself. And even when it looked like he'd left that behind, it was only to turn around and leave Larkin without a word of warning.

I wanted to think he'd changed, but it was hard to trust him.

"No." She frowned. "Well, not this, at least."

I furrowed my brow as Larkin pulled her phone from her purse. "What's going on?"

"I got these texts . . ." Her fingers flew over the phone screen as she spoke. "The first one freaked me out, but I didn't recognize the number and I figured it was maybe a mistake. Like it was meant for someone else. But then I got these yesterday." She held up her phone.

I skimmed the text bubbles on the screen.

I saw you with him.

You're a terrible mother.

You trusted a drug dealer with Diego.

I shivered at the words in spite of the warmer than usual air. When I looked up at her, I knew exactly why she'd looked so troubled. "Why didn't you say anything? Who could it be?" My mind flew to every person we knew.

"I don't know," she said, looking down at her phone again. "It has to be someone in town, right? Because how else would they know all this stuff?" Her voice choked a little.

She looked so small and afraid. I took a couple of steps forward until I could hug her. "It's going to be okay. We'll figure it out."

I stood back, keeping my hands on her arms until she nodded.

"I thought about blocking the number . . . But then what if he—or she—gets mad and . . . and . . ." She wrapped her arms around herself.

I took in a deep breath. "Okay, so it's probably someone who's jealous that Nick's hanging around. What about guys you've dated?" But even as I asked the question, I knew the answer.

Larkin hadn't really dated at all since Diego was born.

"I only went out with that guy who worked at the café a couple of times. But then he moved back to Missoula. And other than that . . ." She shrugged. There was no one else.

I chewed my lip as I thought. The chickens squawked behind me. "What if it's a woman?" There was more than one woman in town who'd had plenty of unwanted opinions on Larkin's pregnancy. As much as I loved Bent Creek, it was still a small town. And people talked.

Larkin pressed her lips together for a moment, and then shook her head. "I mean, the only people I remember who had something to say about me got over it pretty quick once Diego was born. Even Mrs. Cowley slips Diego a cookie when she thinks I'm not watching."

I had to smile at that. Mrs. Cowley had taken the front pew in the church every Sunday since before I could remember, and she wasn't quiet about her opinions.

Larkin sighed. "I don't know. Maybe I should block the number."

"No. Just in case." I paused. "Do you think you should show the police?"

"It's nothing threatening, though. Just someone being mean and trying to freak me out. I think Chief Torrance would take one look at these and tell me there's nothing he can do."

Larkin's phone beeped, and my heart jumped in response.

She glanced at it. "Just my mom," she said with a note of relief in her voice. "She's supposed to be resting, but she's complaining about her co-worker again. And . . . trying to fix me up with a doctor. Again."

"Hmm." I crossed my arms and tapped my fingers against my upper arm. "You ought to take her up on that doctor."

"Why don't I tell her that *you* want to go out with that doctor? Ditch Gabe and all." She shot me a teasing look before she went back to texting.

The roar of a truck sounded from the driveway. "Speaking of which, Gabe's here."

"I'll walk with you." Larkin finished typing and dropped her phone back into her purse.

I waved at Gabe when we reached the driveway. "Going in to wash my hands!"

He nodded as he leaned back against the door of his truck. He could come in. I made it perfectly clear to Luke that if I lived here too, I could invite in whoever I want—including Gabe. Or even Nick, if I felt really crazy. But Gabe never really relaxed when he was here, and it was just easier if we went somewhere else. Most of the time, I offered to meet him, just to avoid Luke stomping around the house in silent rage.

Larkin followed me inside and waited by the door. "Is he taking you out to dinner?" she asked as I dried my hands.

"We'll probably just grab some fast food down by the interstate." I padded down the hallway in my socks to find shoes that didn't have mud caked on the soles.

"Romantic," she shouted after me.

I laughed. Maybe Wendy's wasn't exactly romantic, but hamburgers didn't need to make my heart skip a beat or make me forget how to breathe. Gabe did that without any need for help from food.

"What's on your menu tonight? Mac and cheese? Dino nuggets?" I asked from the hallway as I slipped on a pair of flats while walking.

"Yeah, probably all of the above. Plus green beans. Diego's really into green beans lately." She smiled, but it slowly dropped away the closer we got to her car. I paused beside it as she opened the door and tossed her purse inside. "Hey. Let me know if you get any more of those texts, okay?"

"I will." She held on to the door a moment before sliding into the seat. "Maybe it's just a prank."

"Maybe." And as I walked to Gabe's truck and let him take me into his arms, I hoped with everything I had that it *was* someone's awful idea of a joke.

Larkin had enough on her plate without dealing with some messed-up stalker.

Chapter Fourteen

Nick

I scanned through the microfilm, dull black and white pages blurring before my tired eyes.

Leaning back into the hard, wooden chair provided by the county courthouse, I ran a hand over my face. One day, rural Montana would join the rest of the world with putting stuff like this on the internet.

But for today, it was deeds on microfilm, like they'd done it since 1957.

I blinked several times before turning the knob again. A few minutes into the tedious work, it paid off once more.

Two hundred forty acres, several miles south of Bent Creek, sold to Maple Sun, LLC three years ago.

I sent a copy to the printer, picked it up, and added it to the small stack I'd created over the course of four hours. Flipping through the pages, I added them up. Two properties sold to Maple Sun. Three to Aspen Star, LLC. One to Oak Orbit, LLC. And two to Chestnut Moon, in addition to our ranch and the new one Kyle Clemmons told Gabe about. All within the past ten years.

They were easy enough to spot once I figured out the naming convention. Then it was like they were throwing themselves at me, just waiting to be found.

"Who are you? And why do you need so much land?" I whispered to the sheets of paper.

They didn't say anything back, but the woman at the desk did. "Closing up in ten minutes."

"I'm done." I leaned over to quickly glance through the rest of the microfilm roll. No more tree and space-named companies caught my eye. I rewound the film, gathered my stuff, and thanked the woman.

Outside, the sun was low in the western sky. It was forty-five minutes' drive back to Bent Creek. I'd make it back before dark. As I started the truck, I wondered where Larkin might be. Probably home by now, taking care of Diego. I should've asked for her number. But what would I say if I texted?

Hey. Great to stare into your eyes yesterday. Want to meet up for dinner?

She'd probably throw coffee at me again—and on purpose this time.

I should've gone by the B&B to show Gabe the copies I made. But as I drew up to the intersection at Quarter Mile Road, I took a right instead. I didn't know if it was some old instinct that sent me to the ranch, or if some part of me simply wanted to be there.

When I pulled into the driveway, the sun had set, casting an orange glow over the land and the abandoned buildings—and Larkin's car.

Well, that was interesting.

I opened the truck door and walked slowly up the driveway. The remaining patches of snow crunched under my feet as I approached her car.

It was empty.

"I'm up here."

Following the sound of her voice, I found her on the front porch of the house. She'd moved to the steps, where she stood with her arms crossed.

"What are you doing here?" I asked as I strode across the yard.

She leaned against the porch post. "I could ask you the same thing."

"I don't know." I paused at the bottom of the steps. "I thought I'd go see Gabe . . . but I came here instead."

She was silent a moment, her eyes sweeping past me, out toward what used to be fields and grazing land. "It's a good place to think."

I climbed the steps slowly and turned to follow her gaze. "Yeah. It always was." The warm tones of dusk illuminated everything in gold, making the entire scene feel cozy.

Like home.

A sadness clenched my heart. I *missed* this. This place. This feeling. Family. Home. If I closed my eyes, I could take myself back. The longing was almost overwhelming—the desire to go back in time and experience *having* it again. Just for a little while, just long enough to appreciate it this time.

"I didn't think I'd ever come back here," Larkin said, drawing my attention back to her. She'd dropped her arms and was leaning her head and shoulder against the post. "After . . ."

After I'd left her. I swallowed the guilt. She'd come back after the shooting, terrified and yet trusting. I took it, like I took everything. And I'd broken that trust with no explanation.

She was watching me, those soft eyes seemingly seeing into my mind. "That night with the gunshots scared me. But it was nothing compared to what I had yet to live through."

"Larkin." Nothing I could say would ever be good enough. But I owed it to her—and to myself—to try. I owed her everything. "I'm sorry. It's not enough, and it's too late, I know. But I was wrong, and I need you to know that I realize that now. I think I knew it all along, but I was selfish. I thought you'd be better off, and you probably were, but you didn't deserve me making that decision for you. So . . . I'm sorry. I wish I could give you more."

Her eyes grew shiny, and she blinked quickly as she looked down. "Thank you," she finally said as she looked back up at me. She gave me a sad smile. "I waited a long time to hear that."

She tucked that strand of hair behind her ear. It was such a familiar gesture, one I'd seen her do hundreds of times. At school. After my football games. On this porch. I cleared my throat. "Do you ever wish you could go back in time? Relive the good times, but really appreciate them for what they are? Make better choices and do things right?" My voice came out heavier than I expected, all that longing bursting through the seams of it.

"Sometimes." Larkin's eyes traced my face, and I would have done anything to know what she thought when she looked at me like that. "But then I realize that everything happened the way it did for a reason. If it hadn't, I wouldn't have Diego."

It struck me then, how rich her life had been without me. I'd gone on to do nothing while she became a mother.

But it wasn't too late, was it? I was doing something now. I didn't know what, exactly, but things were changing. I could feel it inside, even if I couldn't name it.

"But sometimes I wish . . ." She paused and looked away, out over the darkening fields.

"What?" My heart clenched while I waited for an answer.

She swallowed visibly, but she didn't look back at me. "Will—Diego's father—and I . . . we weren't together very long. He seemed like the real thing. Steady work, nice to my mom, all that.

He'd come here from California to work construction at the resorts. I thought that maybe I'd finally lucked out. We hadn't even made it a year when I found out about Diego. When I told Will, he acted like he was excited. That we'd be a family. And then the next day . . . he was just gone."

Her words twisted in my gut. "Like me."

"Yes." She looked up at me then. "But no. You broke my heart, Nick Harker, but after all these years, I know it was because *you* were broken. It had nothing to do with me. And . . ."

A moment passed. "And?" I could barely get the word out.

She smiled then, just ever so slightly, and lifted a hand to my face. I fought to breathe normally, to keep my hands where they were, as her fingers traced my jaw. "If Diego had happened with you, you would have stayed."

She was right. It wouldn't have been a question, no matter how broken I was. All I could do was nod as her fingers stilled along my jawline.

"Sometimes I wish it had happened like that. That you were Diego's dad." She bit her lip like she'd said too much and drew her hand away. "I'm sorry. That's . . . a lot to put on you."

I grabbed hold of her wrist and shook my head. "It's not." I didn't know what I was saying, but I knew Diego deserved better than what he got. Larkin deserved better.

Larkin's gaze held mine. Her pulse jumped under my hand. All I had to do was pull her toward me. One second, maybe two until she was flush against me and I could bend down and kiss the worry from her lips. Drive it from her mind until all she knew, all she wanted, all she thought about—was me.

I waited for a moment. Waited for a sign from her that it shouldn't happen.

Her lips parted, her eyes still on me, and that was all the invitation I needed.

Chapter Fifteen

Larkin

One second, I'd been still, my heart beating so hard I was sure that Nick heard every swish and thump. And the next, he'd pulled me so close that I couldn't remember ever being apart from him. Before I could even comprehend what was happening, his lips were on mine, teasing them apart. His hand moved from my wrist to thread its way through my hair. And I was *gone*.

I'd slipped back in time. Or maybe no time had passed at all. Whatever it was, the feel of him against me thrilled me from the tips of my hair down to my toes. That's the way it had always been with Nick. Kissing him was like throwing myself over a cliff, losing every sense and thought and emotion in him—in us.

I didn't think. I couldn't think. All I could do was feel. As one of his hands dropped down my back toward my waistband, some far-off part of me knew this was what I'd been missing for years. It was as if a part of me had been lost, and now it was found.

And I was greedy with the exhilaration of finding it again, of piecing myself back together with Nick. I clung to him like a vine to a wall, pushing myself against him and drinking in the warmth of his body against the cold of the enveloping night.

It wasn't until he'd backed me up against the post that something jarred loose in my head.

Diego.

My son. I couldn't do this. I'd promised myself. "Nick." My voice came out in a breathy whisper as I pulled back.

Nick immediately went to my neck, dropping kisses as he mistook my reticence as asking for more. My eyes closed involuntarily, and I shivered at the press of his lips against my skin. My head swam. I didn't want this to stop. Ever.

My phone buzzed in my pocket, pulling me back to where I needed to be. *Diego.* I had to focus on Diego. "Nick," I said again, more urgently this time as I slid sideways to put some space between us.

"What's wrong? Did I hurt you?" He dropped his hands from my waist and stepped back as he searched my face, entirely serious about the possibility that his kiss could have somehow hurt me.

That was impossible. Aside from making it that much harder for me to back away.

"No. Um . . . my phone." It was a lame excuse, one I punctuated by pulling my phone from my pocket. *I'm afraid I might fall for you only for you to leave me again and break my child's heart too,* wasn't exactly something I wanted to say out loud.

He nodded. "Of course. Diego."

I blinked at him, wondering if my thoughts somehow showed on my face. Until he pointed at my phone, and I realized he meant that I should check and make sure the message wasn't about Diego.

As I lifted it, I hoped with all my strength that it was simply Mom, wondering when I'd be home or asking me to grab some milk on my way.

What's the matter? Too ashamed to reply?

It felt as if the world was caving in around me as I stared at the words on the screen. I wanted to scream at it, to call the number and demand to know who it was and what they wanted. But I didn't. Instead, I clicked the phone off with trembling fingers and shoved it back into my pocket.

"Larkin?' Nick's eyes appeared dark blue in the hazy night. "Is something wrong?"

I swallowed, thinking for just a second about showing the texts to Nick. But I couldn't. Not when whoever it was had said such awful things about him. Nick wasn't a bad person. He never had been, even when he'd thought he was helping his family for that short while back in high school.

He didn't deserve to see that some people had never changed their minds about him. I couldn't hurt him like that, not now. Especially not after he'd given me the apology I'd been waiting so long to hear.

I loved him too much for that.

"Was it your mom? Is something wrong? If you can't drive, I can give you a ride." He was reaching for me now, a strong hand that I could so easily grab on to.

All my feelings—my realization that I still loved him—rose up inside, crashed against the fear lingering from that text, and tears welled up. I swallowed a great, gulping sob, and backed away. Down the steps. And then I turned and ran to my car, leaving Nick standing bewildered behind me.

"Larkin!" His confusion bit through my soul. I shut the door and tried not to look at him as I turned on the car and backed around his truck.

On the road, I pressed the accelerator down and let the hum of the engine guide my thoughts as I wiped away the tears.

I love him.
I don't trust him.
I can't hurt him.
I can't let him hurt us.
I love him.
I'm scared.

Chapter Sixteen

Nick

Mrs. Dowling greeted me with an old spiral-bound notebook
and a narrow gaze. "You look familiar."

I shut the door to the B&B behind me, vaguely remembering that
Gabe had mentioned the older woman had memory issues. "I'm Nick
Harker, Mrs. Dowling. You're known me since I was a kid."

"Nick Harker." She said my name carefully, pronouncing each
syllable as if she was thinking hard about each one. "Yes. Tom's son."

I nodded. It was the first time anyone I'd run into in Bent Creek had
mentioned Pops by name. Hearing it both set me on edge and made
me want to lean in to hear more. I supposed no matter how mad I
was Pops—and I'd been carrying that around for a long time—he was
always my father. And stopping the ranch, seeing Gabe, being back
here, made his absence more . . . real.

"Tom's staying here, you know. Top of the stairs. Room five."

Disappointment swept away any hope of hearing any old stories or fond memories Mrs. Dowling might have tucked away. If I

hadn't known she lapsed into thinking Gabe was Pops on occasion, it would've sent me spinning.

Instead, I just said, "Thanks, Mrs. Dowling. I'll head up there now to see him."

"Yes," she said, nodding as I crossed to the staircase. "I oughtn't tell you this, but maybe you can talk some sense into him. He shouldn't be carrying on with young Miss Creason like that. Not with that little boy she has. And so soon after Amy's accident." She shook her head.

I gripped the banister. Amy had been my mother's name. Miss Creason was Katrina, Gabe's mom. My stepmom. Hearing their names spoken out loud sliced a fresh cut in my heart.

Mrs. Dowling was watching me, waiting for some sort of reply to her lost-in-twenty-years-ago ramblings. All I could do was nod before turning and running up the stairs.

I took a second outside Gabe's room to catch my breath. This was a lot of the past sneaking up on me when I wasn't expecting it. All of Bent Creek was heavy with what had been, but I'd found it easy enough to shove it off to the side—until I was forced to reckon with it.

I knocked on Gabe's door. "Let's get out of here," I said the second he answered.

"Hey to you too. Where do you want to go?"

I shrugged and shoved my hands into my pockets. "Anywhere but this place. The reserve?"

"All right." Gabe looked at me a second with a puzzled look.

"Mrs. Dowling was having a moment. In the past," I said by way of explanation.

Thankfully, Gabe knew exactly what that meant. "Got it. Let me grab my coat."

It was only a few blocks to the reserve, which was a generous description for what was basically a large chunk of land belonging to the town, which no one had done anything with beyond paving a big walking track.

"I've got the papers in my truck," I said, blinking into the cold air. So much for yesterday's warmth. It was dry at least, with no new snow. But I could feel the cold down into my bones. "If you want to see them."

"Yeah, I guess so. Maybe there's something there that'll give me some kind of clue about what to do next. I looked up all those companies. They're all registered here, in Montana. All in good standing. All with the same attorney's office for a registered agent."

"Maybe we could get in touch with that lawyer, then?" A moment too late, I realized I'd said *we*. I was committing myself even more to this dream of Gabe's. I could leave, let him take it from here. Stop trying to prove myself to Larkin. Go back to my anonymous life in Texas where no one cared what my last name was.

It would be easy.

But I was still here. I could make all kinds of excuses, but I wanted to know who it was that had bought the ranch. And now all these other properties—and why.

And I wanted Larkin. More than I should. More than I had any right to.

"That's a good idea." Gabe looked at me expectantly.

"I'd do it," I said. "But you're better on the phone." I shouldn't encourage it, but the curiosity was driving me crazy. The whole thing was a bad idea. No one wanted us here. And if this actually succeeded somehow, and old man Noble found out . . . I sucked in a lungful of cold air. I was getting ahead of myself. All we were doing was calling a lawyer's office to see if we couldn't solve this puzzle.

Gabe was quiet for a moment, and the silence of a Bent Creek morning settled around us. But it didn't make me feel as restless as it had in the days after I'd first arrived here. Maybe because I'd already been hit with the past in every direction, I could relax. Now, the silence felt like living in a cocoon, as if the mountains and the trees held me in their palm. It wasn't bad, I had to admit. It was oddly comforting.

"How's Larkin?" Gabe broke the silence with the one question I couldn't answer.

I shrugged. "I don't know," I answered truthfully. I wish I could've said *Great!* And I would have, if last night had ended differently.

I felt Gabe's eyes on me. If there was anyone in this world I could trust, it was him. Despite the distance we'd put between ourselves when we'd left here, he was my brother and my closest friend. "I went by the ranch last night, and she was there."

To his credit, Gabe didn't look surprised. It was easy to remember why we'd always been so close. Nothing shook him, nothing I ever said made him flinch or look at me different. So I plowed ahead.

"We talked some, and, well, things progressed." I kept my eyes on the bare trees and slate gray sky ahead, trying not to relive that moment for the thousandth time. "She backed off to read a text, and then she left without saying anything." I frowned at the pavement. "She looked upset. I don't know if it was about Diego or what." *And she wouldn't tell me.* That's what bothered me the most. But it shouldn't. After all, why should she trust me?

Gabe frowned, lost in thought for a minute. "She and Marybeth have been thick as thieves lately. Whispering about something, looking at their phones." His frown turned rueful. "At first, I thought it was about us."

I couldn't help but laugh about that as I smacked him on the shoulder. "You wish."

"I think it's something else. I'll ask Marybeth about it."

I nodded, trying not to let on how much his girlfriend's name made my skin crawl.

"How was the ranch? I haven't been out there in a while."

I glanced up at Gabe to see if he was asking more than he'd put into words, but his face held the question honestly.

"A mess."

"Yeah." His voice had a wistful tone as he looked out past the track toward the stand of evergreens that lent a little color to the gray and white world around us. "I think that's why I haven't gone out there lately. It hurts to see it like that, you know?"

"Like a knife to the gut. I'd like to have words with whoever's behind this Chestnut Moon."

"You and me both."

I let the anger seethe for a moment. It felt good to let it boil instead of bottling it up like I'd gotten used to doing. "That place should've been ours. Our birthright."

"Your birthright." There was a note of longing in his voice.

I stopped and turned to look my brother in the eye. "Yours too. You grew up there. You bled for that place as much as any of us, and lost everything. If anyone ever says different, they won't like what I have to say back."

Gabe laughed a little under a sad smile. "There's the brother I know. Thanks, man." He shoved his hands into his coat pockets. "I don't know why that's been on my mind lately. Guess it's because of how focused I've been on the ranch."

That damn place. It was seeping into my bones again, if it had ever even left. "Being out there last night . . ." I shook my head, but whether I was trying to jar the memories loose or forget them altogether, I didn't know. I drew in a deep breath and let it out. If I couldn't be honest with Gabe, I couldn't be honest with anyone, even myself. "It felt like home, you know? Like there's a part of me out there I'll never get back unless . . ."

"Unless it's ours again," Gabe finished for me.

He felt the same. And I'd finally figured out why he was fighting so hard for it.

"Are you in this with me? For real?" he asked, his eyes locked on me.

Was I? I couldn't lie to him. "Yeah. All the way."

He smiled then, and I realized he had no idea what I meant.

I looked away. He'd brushed off my vague warnings about the danger that came with this endeavor. Danger he was courting even more with Marybeth by his side.

He needed more than vague warnings. He needed the cold, hard truth about the Nobles, or he'd be walking into this blindly.

And I wasn't about to let my brother fall into a trap with stars in his eyes.

Chapter Seventeen

Larkin

NICK CAME BY THE house late, after Diego was in bed. But early enough for Mom to fix me with a look that was somewhere between disappointment and sadness.

I couldn't deal with her expectations at the moment, not with those texts and my mixed-up feelings about Nick. As I peered through the window at his truck, I realized the only way he had to contact me was to find me in person. I hadn't offered him my number, and he hadn't asked. I guess that might've been something I found disappointing, but instead it seemed . . . thoughtful. He was being careful with me, not intruding on my time, keeping enough distance to let me think.

Distance. I gave a half-smile to the door as I approached it. There wasn't any distance between us last night—until I claimed it. I closed the door behind me, Mom still hovering in the kitchen. I knew she'd be watching us through the window as she pretended to dry dishes.

I slipped on the jacket I'd grabbed from the pegs near the door as I waited for Nick to get out of his truck. I'd probably freaked him out when I ran off like that last night. And instead of running away himself, he was here.

I didn't know what to make of that.

I crossed my arms and walked down the driveway. The farther away from the house we were, the less likely Mom was going to overhear anything.

"Hey," he said, leaning against the side of his truck.

Why did he have to look so good doing something so *normal*? He'd left his hat inside the truck, and his dark hair swept back in the wind that had blown down the mountains. His eyes were a soft gray in the porch light, and even though he was wearing a coat, I'd never forget the feel of the muscles that lined his arms and shoulders.

"Hey." I looked down at the driveway to force those thoughts from my mind.

"I wanted to check on you, after . . ." He trailed off as I looked up. "Are you all right?"

No. I realized I'm still in love with you, but I can't be because of Diego, and by the way, I'm getting creepy texts from some stalker weirdo.

"Yeah." It was a lie from ten different directions, and Nick clearly recognized it with the way his mouth twitched downward.

He rubbed a hand across his chin as he stood up straight. A reckless, wild part of me wished he'd just take two steps, wrap his arms around me, and force all the doubts from my mind.

"Larkin, if something's wrong, you can tell me."

It would be so easy to pull out my phone, show him those texts, and let him take over. He would, I knew it. He'd make it so I didn't have to worry anymore.

But those words . . . I couldn't gut him like that. Nick was anything but weak, but all that stuff that happened with his family—there was a reason he'd left. And if he'd managed to put himself back together, I wasn't going to whip out some awful allegations about his past to tear him back down.

Which meant I had to handle that on my own.

"Everything's fine." I forced a smile.

He watched me a moment, and I knew he didn't buy it.

"It's me," he said. "I'm sorry. I shouldn't have burst back into your life like this. I—"

"No!" I'd moved toward him without realizing it. "Nick, it's not . . . it's not you. It's . . ." I had to be honest, at least partially. "It's Diego."

The wind whipped my hair into my face, and I brushed it out of my eyes, remembering how Nick had done that for me at the coffee shop not so long ago. I couldn't let my mind go there, let myself get lost in him again—not if I was going to make him understand why I had to be so careful.

"Diego's a great kid. I liked spending time with him. If you think it bothers me that you have him, I promise you it doesn't. In fact . . ." He smiled, wrapping himself around my heart again. "I can't imagine you without him."

My throat ached with emotion. He didn't know just how much that meant to me. Just how many guys had started to show interest only to back off once I mentioned Diego. The fact I hadn't really dated since Will had just as much to do with that as it did with me being wary. Diego and I were a package deal, and there weren't many men my age who understood that.

But Nick did.

I let out my breath. Nick didn't know just how much easier he'd made it for me to say what I needed. "Then you understand why I'm cautious. I want to give my son more than I had. He deserves it—he deserves everything. And I already failed at that once when his dad left."

"That wasn't your fault. You didn't fail at anything." Nick's eyes darkened to steel.

It warmed my heart, but I shook my head. "No, maybe not. But I wish I'd known. I wish I could have chosen better." I paused, gathering courage for what I needed to say next. "Everything I do—every choice I make—it affects him. I grew up with a dad who left. Diego's dad already left, before he even met him. I can't let him get close to someone only to have that person leave." Tears pooled in my eyes, and I pressed the back of my sleeve-covered hand to them.

Nick regarded me for a moment, not saying anything, and—thankfully—not reaching for me. I felt fragile, like I'd just laid my soul bare for him, showing him my deepest fears. I didn't know what he'd do with it, but if he touched me right now, I'd probably crumble into a million pieces.

"I get it," he finally said, his voice low and sure. "And I agree. But Larkin?"

I pressed my lips together as I wrapped my arms tighter against myself. "Yeah?"

"I won't leave. Not like I did before. I need you to know that."

I didn't react. "How do you know for sure?"

He glanced away, off toward where the road wound around a bend and made its way out of town into a pothole-ridden dirt trail. "You said I was broken then. You were right. I was young, and everything with my father, the ranch, his . . . business—it tore me in two. I couldn't see any way out except to be somewhere else." He closed his eyes for a moment, the silence humming around us. From somewhere inside, probably just by the window, a pot clanged against the sink.

"What if that happens again?" I said, my voice barely a whisper.

He looked at me then, his jaw set and his arms at his side. "It won't. I promise you that, Larkin. I can handle things better now. I should've talked to you about it back then. Taken you with me."

"I was sixteen. I couldn't just *leave*."

He rubbed his forehead and nodded. "You're right. But I could've told you I was going. Could've kept in touch, could've followed through on all those promises I'd made you. Could've come back for you later."

All those old feelings of being cast aside burned at his remorse. "Why didn't you? I kept hoping you would . . . for so long."

"I was afraid." He looked right in my eyes as he said it, and I knew it was the truth. Whether he was afraid I'd turn him away, afraid of coming back here, afraid of the Nobles, I didn't know.

But he looked anything but afraid now.

"I'm not the same person I was then. Do you believe me when I say that?"

I wanted to. So badly.

I squeezed my eyes shut, looking for strength. But I didn't find it until I opened them again and saw it reflected in Nick's eyes. He was showing me again and again who he was now.

It was time to shed myself of the past and think of the future. And sometimes, that meant taking a chance, even if it scared me to my very core.

"I do," I said softly. I took a tentative step toward him.

He smiled then, happiness etching every angle and line on his face. He held out his hands and I took them, letting his strength bond with my own.

I had more to say, and this time, I spoke without hesitation. "I need to take things slow, okay?"

"As slow as you want. We have plenty of time."

I tilted my head. "What about Texas? Your job there?"

He shrugged. "It's there if I need it, and if it's not, there are plenty of other opportunities."

I didn't ask if he meant Bent Creek. I wasn't sure if I wanted to know—or if he knew for certain yet.

"I came here for Gabe," he continued. "But I stayed for you. No matter how many dirty looks some of these people give me."

"And the ranch," I said lightly. "You're staying for that too. I saw the way you were looking at that land last night."

He lifted a shoulder in a shrug, but I knew. There was a piece of him here he couldn't shake, no matter how far away he ran.

He'd turned my palms over and was running his thumbs across them, sending shivers up my arms and down my back. "Does it count as slow if I ask you before I kiss you?"

His sincerity made me laugh. "I suppose so. Except my mom is just inside, and I'm pretty sure she's—"

"I don't care who's watching."

And suddenly, I didn't either. I pulled my hands from his, took his face between my palms, and did the asking myself.

I'd surprised him, and something about that surprised even myself. It only took a second for Nick to go from startled to pressing his hands against either side of my waist. My head began to spin with the taste of him, and every doubt I'd had flew away. Why would I ever question something that felt so perfectly right?

He clung to me like he might never hold me again, and that only made me want more. I didn't know how much time passed. Nick's fingers had wound through the loops on my jeans, holding me in place, and my hands pressed against his back as I tried to close every last fraction of an inch.

I was dizzy with him, drunk on his scent and his taste. A low groan sounded from his throat, and I held on to him for all I was worth. He backed away for just a fraction of a second, his eyes dark and consuming.

"Nick," I whispered, and his mouth found mine again, answering what I needed without a word.

What I needed was *him*. So badly that my entire body shook with the wanting. He was a piece of me that I'd lost for so long, and I was greedy with the thought of having it back.

The squeak of a door sounded from somewhere far away. *Mom*.

Chapter Eighteen

Nick

THE SQUEAL OF THE door hinges brought me crashing back down to Earth. With effort, I leaned back, drawing a startled gasp from Larkin's lips. It made me wonder if she'd heard the door at all.

One quick glance up, and there was Jeanine Reyes. With all the anger a woman of her small stature could possess, she aimed it at me. I couldn't question it. After all, I'd left her to pick up the pieces when I ran off to Texas. No wonder she hated me.

Larkin teetered slightly as she backed up against my truck. I steadied her, taking hold of her arm as she grabbed the sideview mirror for balance.

"Okay?" I whispered.

She nodded, and my hand ached to fit against her lower back, offer her support while laying my claim.

Slow. Although that kiss had been anything but slow, I was pretty sure Larkin wouldn't thank me for any purposeful public display of affection in front of her mother.

"It's cold out here," Jeanine said as she stepped from the small stoop at the side door.

I hadn't felt it, not with Larkin anywhere near me. The girl was like a fire, and I craved the heat.

Jeanine paused beside her own car, arms crossed. She said nothing.

"Hi, Jeanine," I said, trying to sound casual. She'd liked me once upon a time. Used to make me pancakes for supper and loved coming to my games when she didn't have to work. I searched for something neutral to say. Larkin had mentioned her mom had found a new job at the hospital a little while ago. "Congratulations on your job."

Jeanine didn't acknowledge my words. Instead, she continued to level me with a look that could have withered flowers. "It's getting colder," she said to her daughter without taking her eyes from me. "We should go inside, Larkin."

She couldn't have made it any clearer that I wasn't welcome. I couldn't blame her, but it hurt just the same. I suppose some small part of me had hoped she would see how much I cared about her daughter.

Larkin looked up at me sheepishly, as if she were a teenager getting caught with a boy after curfew. "Thanks for coming by."

"Mama?" Diego's voice was faint, but his face was clear, pressed up against the glass of the screen door.

"Coming, baby." With a last, quick smile at me, Larkin walked quickly toward the house.

The second the door shut behind her, Jeanine turned her attention back to me.

I fished my keys from my pocket. "It was good to see you," I said, trying to bury the awkwardness of the situation with friendliness. No way had she missed what we'd been up to in her driveway.

"Nick." Her voice was flat yet edged with the sharpness of a knife.

I paused, my hand on the door. "Yeah?"

"Don't come back here. I'd tell you to stay away from my daughter if I thought it would do any good. But I don't want to see you at my house."

Every inch of me wanted to bite back. To tell her Larkin was an adult capable of making her own decisions. But my temper had never gotten me anywhere but in trouble, so I held my tongue. "I'm sorry you feel that way," I said evenly. "If it does any good, you should know I'm a different person now than I was at eighteen."

"I'm not sure I believe that. You would've showed up before now, before your brother came back to town. I don't know what you're up to, but I suspect it's a path that leads to nothing good."

My heart clenched as my fingers dug into the door handle. Back when everything went sideways, Larkin's mom had been on my side. She'd taken other people to task who'd questioned how involved me or my brothers had been. She'd stood up for me, even when I didn't deserve it.

I guessed that now I knew what it felt like to be on Jeanine Reyes's bad side.

"I promise you, it's all fine. I'm helping Gabe figure out how to buy back our ranch."

She held her gaze slow and steady. "You understand it's hard for me to believe a word that comes out of your mouth. When you left, you took every bit of trust I had in you. You were like a son to me, but now . . . Now I wonder how much of the old gossip was true. If people were laughing behind my back when I defended you."

I opened my mouth to reassure her, but she stepped back and dropped her arms. "You can go now," she said. "I have nothing more to say to you."

I forced back righteous anger. It tasted like bile, burning my throat as I climbed into the truck and backed out of the driveway.

How many other people felt the same way? No one else had stood up for me, not like Jeanine. But I was sure that most of the people I passed every day thought the same things about me. Gabe had somehow found his place here again, and maybe, for a bright shining second, I thought I could too.

But could I really? Even if by some miracle we got the ranch back, would this town ever feel like home again?

I pulled up at the four-way stop where Larkin's street met Main Street. It was deserted this time of night. Any nighttime small-town action took place at the little bars at Third and Pine, Bent Creek Strike and Spare, or the four-screen theater that was barely hanging on in the twenty-first century on the outskirts of town. I leaned against the steering wheel, my eyes on the empty street. I could almost see the ghosts of the past again, as I had when I'd first ventured up here.

This town was mine too. I had a history here, not all of it bad. Running was easy, but I was tired of running. I wanted to remember the good times.

I wanted to make more of them.

I didn't know whether I could do that here—not yet. But what I did know was that I wouldn't give up my corner of this town's memory without a fight.

I had to show them who I really was. Who I'd become. I wasn't that moody Harker kid who happened to be decent at football. The one they'd rightly suspected had spent a little time involved in the illegal family business. The one who left when things got too hard.

I was more than that. I was the big brother who made sure everything was okay for his younger brothers. I was the one who organized more than one volunteer activity for the football team. I was the guy who got himself out of the drug business and did all he could to get his younger brother out too.

I was the one who came back.

And I sure wasn't leaving yet—not until I proved myself to this town.

Chapter Nineteen

Marybeth

Running late. Be there soon.

I put a hand over my mouth to keep from laughing at the kissy emoji Gabe used after his text. He wasn't the emoji type—at all. But I stopped laughing when his next text popped up.

Nick stopping by. Tell him to wait for me, ok?

I made a face at my phone as I texted back a simple *Ok*. What in the world could Nick need before Gabe and I went out that he couldn't get just by texting or calling his brother?

I'd just flipped the sign on the door from *Open* to *Closed* when I spotted Nick. I squinted through the glass as he ran after Mrs. Cowley, handing her a glove she must have dropped. They talked for a moment, which was a surprise. I was pretty sure Mrs. Cowley had strong opinions about Nick, just as she did about everything in town. They finished, and I ducked out of the way before Nick could see me watching.

He knocked on the door, and I drew in a calming breath before plastering a smile on my face. Thinking of Nick helping Mrs. Cowley did the trick—it was a kindness I had yet to see from him. Now if only Nick could show that same kindness toward me. Gabe had no idea that his brother seemed bent on driving us apart—and if it were up to me, he'd never know. The last thing I wanted was us coming between him and his family.

"Hey, Nick," I said as genuinely as possible as I opened the door to let him in.

If I ever thought Gabe looked out of place in my shop, it was nothing compared to his stepbrother. I was itching to grab that Santa hat I'd thought about sticking on him the first time he'd come in here. Nick was just as big as Gabe, the tip of his hat scraping the faux pine boughs I had hanging from the ceiling, but his regular expression in Bent Creek Christmas was a scowl. If he had the power, he'd probably bring in rain clouds to drench all my hard work.

"What are you up to?" I asked pleasantly as I tidied the Christmas kitchen towel display. "Did you see Larkin?"

"Yeah. Just came from there."

I moved to the hot chocolate station to grab the Crock Pot insert and spotted the flash of a smile. So there was something that made Nick Harker happy—and that something was Larkin. Despite my reservations about his intentions, I liked seeing that she made him as happy as he made her. She'd told me he'd changed—and I hoped she was right.

Because unlike Nick, I wasn't about to insert myself between them to try and push them apart.

"She's got a lot to say about you lately," I said over my shoulder as I walked to the back room to empty and clean the Crock Pot.

"Yeah?" He'd followed me, waiting at the doorway.

I bit my lip to keep from smiling as I scrubbed. Nick was clearly a softie where Larkin was concerned. "Mostly good," I said.

"Mostly?" He'd leaned against the doorframe, his eyebrows crooked up into a question.

"All good lately," I confessed as I grabbed a towel.

He smiled at that. It was like some other man had come and taken over his body. He actually looked somewhat friendly. It reminded me of how he was in high school, when he and Larkin were together but before everything had started falling apart during his senior year.

I set the towel down, thinking. If he believed that he and Larkin deserved happiness after everything he'd put her through—if he believed he was worthy of forgiveness—then why didn't he see that he was still holding the past against Gabe and me?

Suddenly, I had to know.

"Can I ask you a question?" I crossed my arms, decided that looked too defensive, and uncrossed them.

He said nothing, just raised those eyebrows again.

I chewed on my lip a second before plowing forward. "Why are you trying so hard to break up Gabe and me?"

He didn't expect that, at least not so directly. I could tell from the way his eyes widened slightly and how he busied himself with pushing off the doorframe to stand up straight.

"I know you got into Larkin's head, convincing her that I'm somehow dangerous to Gabe." I paused, letting the absurdity of that sink in. "So if Larkin can set your past aside and give you another chance, shouldn't that be true for me and Gabe?"

"It's not the same thing," he said, a dark edge shading the previous lightness to his voice.

"How? You deserve forgiveness, but things you blame my dad for—something I'm not even responsible for—don't?"

"Larkin knows what she's getting with me. I've been honest. Which is more than I can say for your family. I don't trust you—any of you."

He stood like a rock in the doorway, a solid chunk of barely contained anger, hard eyes regarding me under the shadow of his hat.

I put my hands on my hips. If Nick Harker thought he was intimidating me, he thought wrong. I didn't grow up with five brothers for nothing. I held his gaze and gave him a searing one of my own. "I've never done anything to make you second-guess why I'd want to be with Gabe. You're judging me on my last name, when I had nothing to do with whatever issues your dad had with mine. I was a kid, like you. Like Larkin."

He laughed then, short and anything but sweet. "Like your brother?"

I dug my nails into my palms, trying to figure out which brother he meant. "You'll have to be more specific."

"Luke." He waited, like I should have understood everything in that one word.

Luke had been in the same class as Nick and Gabe, but they definitely weren't ever friends. As far as I was aware, they'd steered clear of each other.

"Oh, come on, Marybeth." Nick's voice had gone sickly soft, like a snake waiting to pounce on its prey. "You weren't that naïve."

I bristled at the accusation. "I don't know what you're talking about."

He watched me a moment, and just as I thought I would explode from the not knowing, he said, "You don't know what Luke did."

It wasn't a question. My curiosity shot up like a flag. He believed me . . . but what sort of awful thing was he about to throw at me?

Nick shoved his hands into his pockets and glanced over his shoulder. No one was there—Gabe hadn't arrived yet. All that was behind him was a joyful array of Christmas goods, a lingering scent of chocolate and peppermint, and Nat King Cole on the speakers. He looked back at me almost cautiously, as if I were a horse he didn't want to spook.

Luke was my brother. I'd taken care of him, taken care of the ranch for him, when he couldn't do more than drag himself out of bed and stare at the wall. I'd never seen anyone as broken as he was after Liz had died, not even Larkin after she'd been abandoned a second time. Whatever Nick was about to say, it couldn't be that bad—because Luke simply wasn't capable of it.

"He was in that car." Nick's voice was void of emotion.

I shook my head in confusion. "What car?"

His eyes never left my face. It was as if he was assessing my every reaction. "The one that showed up at our ranch that night. The one that opened fire on me, my dad, my brother, Larkin."

I blinked at him. His words might have been in Japanese for all the sense they made to me. "No."

The word hung between us.

Nick kept watching me, and I tried to school my face. I tried to keep all the emotion inside, somewhere he couldn't see. But it showed in my voice the second I spoke. "That's impossible."

"Is it?"

My mind reeled backward, searching for the answer. "That wasn't . . ." My voice was a whisper, beginning to parrot what I'd overheard Dad say about Mr. Harker's accusations. *That wasn't us.* He'd blamed it on someone else, some Canadians that had come down and were making trouble in town. I didn't care about the specifics then. His explanation was good enough for me, when all my focus was on comforting my best friend. The idea of Dad trying to kill Larkin—or anyone—was ludicrous.

And Larkin had never said anything about Luke. All these years, and she never seemed afraid of him.

"Larkin would have said something." I felt like I was reaching for vines over a slippery ravine, trying to grab on to something that would preserve everything I thought I knew.

"Larkin didn't see."

I bit down on my lip. It made sense. I hated that it made sense. I remembered her eyes shining with unshed tears as she told me how Nick had thrown her to the floor of the porch and laid over top of her, shielding her from the gunshots. She wouldn't have had time to see who was in that car. But Nick . . .

Still, I couldn't believe that of my brother. Luke was the oldest, innately protective and ready to defend any of us should we have needed it. But to willingly join something that awful . . .

If he had, that meant he'd been lying to me for years. That Dad had been lying to me, because there was no way he wouldn't have known about it.

That was impossible.

"Ask him yourself," Nick said shortly. "Then ask him where he got that beating he took a week later."

The memory was right there, hidden under how focused I'd been on Larkin at that time. Luke had come home one night, limping, bruised, and bloody. He refused to say what had happened, and I didn't think anything of it. It hadn't been the first fight Luke had been in, and it wasn't the last. But this one had warranted a trip to the ER, stitches, and a couple of broken ribs.

I glared at Nick then, my mind a swirling mess of emotion. "If you tell me that you and Gabe—"

"Gabe didn't know anything about it. He wasn't there. He'd never wanted to be involved, and I wasn't about to push him into it. I never told him. But maybe that was a mistake." Nick paused. "You tell him. Or I will. He deserves to know that your brother tried to kill me."

He really believed Luke was in that car, that Luke had . . . I couldn't even think it. It was so far from what I knew my brother to be. I couldn't speak. I just stared at Nick as everything he'd said churned around and around in my mind.

It all made sense now, why Nick had pushed so hard for us to break up. He truly thought Luke was dangerous. My mind flitted back to Christmas Eve, when Luke met Gabe outside with his rifle. A sick feeling made me grab on to the edge of the sink.

It wasn't true. It *couldn't* be. But in Nick's mind, Luke was capable of murder. And he probably thought the only reason my brother was tolerating this relationship was to use me to get to Gabe.

"I'll stand by whatever Gabe decides," Nick said. "But he gets to make the decision with all the facts. I'm done with keeping secrets. It isn't who I am anymore."

I barely heard what Nick said. I had to find out the truth from Luke. I had to hear him say it was a ridiculous idea, that Nick had mistook someone else for him. It was the only thing that made sense in the family I knew. The Harkers had been in the wrong back then. Not us.

I moved forward without thinking, pushing past Nick and into my store. I barely remembered to grab my purse.

"Marybeth!" Gabe was just outside the door as I pulled it open.

"I have to go." It was all I could say. I couldn't even look him in the eye. I had to get home. Now.

"Where are you going?" I heard him jog behind me as the cold bit through my sweater. I'd left my coat in the shop.

"I thought we were planning to get a drink, go to the Strike and Spare . . ." He trailed off as he must have realized I wasn't stopping.

"I have to go," I whispered as I unlocked my old Honda and slid inside. I didn't want to see Gabe, not until I knew the truth, but there he was, standing just a few feet away, the sweetest look of concern on his face.

"I love you," I said inside the car, where he couldn't hear me. The words fogged up my windshield.

Whether he'd still feel the same way about me once he heard what Nick thought was true, I didn't know.

Chapter Twenty

Larkin

"Bye, have a good evening."

I shut and locked the door of Mountain Roasters behind Kyle Clemmons and breathed a sigh of relief. I hadn't heard from the anonymous texter in a while, and life felt almost normal. But I was still on edge, just waiting.

It was closing time, though, and so far, no strangers and no texts. Maybe he'd given up. I pulled out my phone, thinking I'd text Marybeth to let her know—when the phone rang in my hand. Her name lit up the screen, and I smiled at the coincidence.

"Hey, I was just getting ready to text you. Are you still at the shop?"

A sniffle came from the other end. "No, I'm home."

I frowned as I took the phone off speaker and leaned against the counter. "What's going on? Is everything okay?"

"It's . . . No." She gulped a sob as I looked around the coffee shop, wondering how fast I could clean up so I could get to the ranch.

"Do you need me? I can be there soon. I just have to clean up a bit. I'll text Mom, and maybe she can bring Diego over."

Marybeth didn't respond right away. I picked up the metal pitcher of skim milk and was just about to say something when she finally spoke. "Larkin, I hate to make you talk about this but . . . That night at the Harkers', sophomore year? With the . . . the gunshots . . ." She sniffed again, and I went still, the handle of the pitcher digging into my palm.

"Yeah . . ." I said carefully. The trauma of that night would always be with me, but somehow, after talking to Nick, it felt as if I'd overcome some hurdle in healing from it.

In healing from everything.

But something in Marybeth's voice made it sound as if this would be a conversation I'd rather not have.

She let out a shuddering breath that reverberated through the phone. "Did you see anyone in the car? The one that drove up."

"No." The memory of that night was so vivid in my mind. I hadn't noticed anything about the car at all, except it had to have been a dark-colored vehicle. "Nick pushed me down before I even heard the first shot. When we got up, they were gone."

"That's what he said." Her voice was soft, as if she were thinking while she spoke.

"Who? Nick?" I couldn't imagine why Nick would be talking about that night with Marybeth. He'd always claimed it was the Nobles—his whole family did. But there was never any evidence, and Mr. Noble denied it up and down. There was no police investigation—there never was with anything involving the Nobles or the Harkers. Until the very end.

"Nick came to my shop," she said, her voice a little less shaky now. She went on to tell me what he'd said. I sat down hard in the closest chair, my free hand gripping the edge of the table as she relayed the information.

"He never said anything to me. Not about Luke." I closed my eyes, searching my memory. Nick had clammed up about the shooting once it became clear that the Nobles weren't going to take responsibility for it. I didn't press it. After all, Marybeth was my best friend, and the bad blood between their families wasn't anything I wanted to be involved in. Besides, it had taken all my effort just to function normally afterward. For months, every time a car drove up beside me, I'd felt paralyzed.

"That's what I was going to ask you." Marybeth sounded disappointed, as if she hoped I could've cleared it all up for her.

"Did you ask Luke about it?"

"He's not here. I will . . . I suppose I was just hoping that maybe . . ."

"I wish I'd seen inside of that car." If I could take away any of Marybeth's doubt about her brother, I would. After all she'd done for him, she deserved the brother she thought she had. "Do you want me to come over? Be moral support when you ask him?"

"No, but thank you." She sighed. "Have you gotten any more texts?"

"Not today," I answered.

"Good. Maybe he lost your number."

I gave a rueful laugh. "I hope so."

We said goodbye and hung up after I insisted I'd text her later to check on her. I started cleaning up again, my mind drifting as I worked. I'd have to talk to Nick about all of this too. Not so much for keeping the information about Luke—or what he thought was Luke—to himself. That I understood, considering how upset I'd been after it had happened.

But why wouldn't he tell me now? And more specifically, why wouldn't he tell me that he was planning to give that information to my best friend?

I knew he was no fan of Marybeth's, especially where Gabe was concerned. But I thought he'd dropped his campaign to convince them that they weren't right for each other. After all, he hadn't said anything about it since asking me to talk to Marybeth. I guessed I'd hoped he'd just decided it wasn't worthwhile, that maybe what he'd found with me again was a much better use of his time.

A raw feeling gnawed at my heart, a little worried but mostly disappointed. I'd thought better of him.

Unless he really thought Luke was a danger to Gabe? That was what he'd indicated when we first talked about it. It seemed ridiculous, knowing who Luke was, but I suppose given that he thought Luke was behind that shooting at the ranch, maybe it wasn't such a far-fetched idea for him.

I frowned at the countertop I'd scrubbed to a gleam. It was useless to worry over it. The only way I was going to get a straight answer—and hopefully reassure myself—would be to ask him directly.

A knock at the door made me jump. But it was only Nick. I grinned. It was as if I'd somehow conjured him here. I held up a finger to tell him to wait a moment while I rinsed out the rag, did a quick glance around the shop, and gathered my coat and purse. The second I stepped outside, he wrapped his arms around my waist, enveloping me in his warmth as I turned to lock the door.

"Hey, you," he said, his breath tickling my ear.

"Hey." I dropped the keys into my pocket and turned in his embrace. I leaned my head back on the door as I looked up into his eyes. They were bright and clear, with nothing angry or secretive to be seen.

"What's wrong?" he asked, clearly noting my hesitation.

"Nothing." I didn't want to talk about it yet. I wanted to savor this moment with him. I ran my hands under his coat, finding the hem of his shirt, and tucked my palms against his skin.

"Larkin." My name was a groan on his lips as he closed his eyes briefly. He opened them again, the heat in the blue making it impossible to look away. "Can I—"

"When I said to go slow, I didn't mean you had to ask me every single time before you kissed me."

"Are you sure?"

I gave him a reproachful look. "Nick—"

I didn't get to finish because he finally did what I wanted him to. For a few blissful moments, I lost myself entirely. The street around us, the coffee shop, everything that worried me fell away under the insistent pressure of his lips against mine. All my mind could hold was the indentation of his fingers against my back, the warmth of his skin against my hands, the tease of his tongue on mine. Nothing could get to me in that moment, and I wanted to live in it forever.

The back of my head bumped gently against the door as Nick pressed closer to me. One hand moved to my cheek, and I thought I would melt right there against the glass, under the flickering streetlight. He held my face as he continued to kiss me, and I never wanted to leave this spot.

The sound of a throat clearing made my eyes flutter open. Nick pulled away, his eyes dazed. It was like waking up from a long nap. I was disoriented and dizzy, and I wasn't sure I even cared who might be nearby. We looked at each other for half a second, both of us breathing hard, before Nick finally turned toward the interruption.

"Gates," Nick said in a thick voice, his hand finally coming away from around my back.

My hands fell away from him, and I straightened before finally looking at my boss. "Hi Charlie, I . . . I closed up." I gestured uselessly at the door as I waited for his tirade.

That look of annoyance I was used to flashed across his face, but it was gone the second he glanced at Nick. All he did was nod and shift the large box in his hands. Another box sat on the sidewalk beside him.

"I just . . . uh . . . I need to get inside. To put these away."

"Oh. Yeah. Of course." I stepped aside, and then fumbled for my key so I could unlock the door for him.

"You need help?" Nick asked from behind me. At first I thought he was asking me, but when I turned, he'd picked up the box from the ground.

"No . . . Okay. Sure, I guess." Charlie's eyes widened, as if he thought Nick might throw the box at him instead of carrying it in.

I waited while Nick followed Charlie inside. They talked briefly, and although I couldn't hear the conversation, it ended with Nick slapping Charlie on the back and Charlie stumbling forward.

"What in the world did you talk to him about?" I asked when Nick emerged.

"Coffee cups."

I blinked at him, and then burst into laughter. "That's one of Charlie's favorite subjects." I paused a moment. "That was nice of you."

Nick looked uncomfortable. "I'm trying."

"Maybe you could convince him to let me use the kitchen and sell some of my cookies and muffins."

"He's a fool if he doesn't take you up on that." Nick held out a hand. "Walk you to your car?"

I slipped my hand into his, and as the silence grew around us, I knew I had to ask the question that had been weighing on my mind.

"Nick?" I started.

"Yeah?" He gripped my hand tighter as we crossed the street.

I swallowed my nerves. "Marybeth called me. Why didn't you tell me about Luke?"

We'd reached my car, and he'd let go of my hand so I could get to my keys. Nick turned to face me, taking his hat off and running a hand through his hair. "She told you about Luke?"

I sighed a little, grateful for not having to say it myself. "Why didn't you tell me?"

He grimaced. "It would've been a lot to put on you back then. You were having a hard time dealing with it, and I didn't want to make it worse. Especially since Marybeth was your friend. Jackson and I dealt with it when we figured out Pops wasn't going to do anything more than issue threats."

He and his brother *dealt with it*. I could feel the blood drain from my face. I vaguely remembered Luke being in the hospital afterward, and Marybeth had mentioned it in passing on the phone earlier.

"It was a long time ago," Nick said softly, reaching for my hand again.

I let him take it. His touch anchored me somehow. And he was right—it was years ago. He'd been younger, more impulsive, and—although I hated to think about it—not that far removed from the work he'd done for his dad. The work I'd never asked him about, because I didn't want to know.

"Marybeth doesn't believe it was Luke in the car," I said.

"I'd swear on my mother's grave that it was. They pulled up right under that light that used to be near the big tree. He looked me right in the eye from the passenger seat."

I swallowed. Nick sounded awfully certain. I had to stay focused—get answers to the questions that had plagued me after Marybeth's call. "Why didn't you let me know you were going to tell Mary-beth?"

He turned my hand over in his. "I didn't know if— I didn't want to mess things up between us. It's family business, and you never wanted anything to do with that. Not that I blame you at all."

"It stops being *family business* when it devastates my best friend. Whatever affects Marybeth affects me too."

A spark of something—irritation, maybe—flashed across his face. It was gone in a second, making me wonder if I'd even seen it. But it triggered some deep down, old feeling—the thought that maybe Nick disliked my friendship with Marybeth. He'd never said it out loud, never even hinted at it. But I'd seen that look before, and part of me wondered if he was keeping his true feelings on that matter hidden.

I plunged ahead, wanting him to understand. "She's the only one, besides my mother, who's always been there for me. She always caught me when everything I thought I had disappeared into dust. I can never repay her for everything she's done for me. That she still does for me."

"I know," he said, his voice strained.

"So, why now? Why dump this on her now?"

He steeled his jaw. "Gabe never knew, and he needs to. I should've told him years ago, but he hated that stuff as much as you did."

I saw nothing in his face to indicate he was only telling me a half-truth, but I still had to ask. "It's not because you're trying to break them up?"

He drew in a deep breath and let it out. "If you'd asked me that a week or two ago, I would've said that it was. But now . . . I don't know what I think. I suppose I'd still prefer it, but I like seeing him happy. He gets to make his own decisions, and I respect that. But he deserves to make them having all the information available. He has no idea what kind of danger he's in. In the end, though, what he chooses isn't up to me."

I watched him a moment. I had no reason not to believe him, and I *wanted* to believe him, even if I thought he was wrong about Luke.

"Okay," I said, threading my fingers through his.

He smiled at me then, honest and joyful, and I was filled with such gratitude that this man was back in my life. Maybe, as my mom had always said, his leaving had been for the best. But for a different reason. Maybe it had allowed him to grow in a way he never could here, so he could return to me a better man.

I wanted to throw my arms around him and tell him how much I still loved him, but I had to remember my own request to take it slow. So instead, I settled for leaning in to give him a quick, chaste kiss before getting into my car.

I rolled down the window far enough to let him lean his arms on it.

"Larkin Reyes, you're like to drive me crazy, you know that?"

"I know." A satisfied feeling flooded me from head to toe as he backed away and I rolled up the window.

I was halfway home, thoughts in the clouds, when my phone buzzed a few times. I picked it up when I got into the driveway, expecting to see news from Marybeth. But I got something else altogether—something that made chills creep up my spine, like a thousand eyes were watching me.

Stubborn and stupid, Larkin.

You should've listened to me.

It's time you knew who you're throwing your life away for.

And why he's really here.

Chapter Twenty-one

Marybeth

THE TIRES OF LUKE'S truck crunched over the gravel and remaining snow in the driveway at 9:07 p.m.

I knew the exact time because I hadn't moved from my chair at the kitchen table since right after I'd talked to Larkin. I'd poured myself a bowl of cereal under the guise of actually eating something for supper, but I hadn't touched it.

I looked at my phone again. 9:08. Another text from Gabe came through, but I didn't answer. Not yet. Not until I knew for sure. All I could hope was that Nick hadn't said anything to Gabe yet. But I didn't want Gabe to worry, so I opened up his texts, and without reading them, I typed out, *I'm ok. Call you soon.*

The side door finally opened, a gust of cold air blowing in after my brother. I left my phone on the table and stood. His arms were full of bags from the grocery store.

"What did you get?" I asked as I took some of the bags from him, momentarily distracted from my worries. I peered into one and saw wrapped packages from the deli and a container of potato salad.

"Food for the ranch hands. For tomorrow."

I wrinkled my forehead as I unpacked the bags and stowed the cold items in the fridge. "What's tomorrow?"

"Nothing. I just wanted to do something for them, especially the guys that have hung on over the past couple of years, you know? Lunch sounded good."

I wadded up one of the plastic bags as I regarded my brother. He was inspecting a tray filled with what looked like microwavable meatballs. I couldn't put two and two together—how could Luke, who was worrying about heating up food for the guys he worked with every day, be the same person Nick claimed he saw in the car that night?

"Why are you looking at me like that?" He'd set the tray down and was eyeing me warily.

I reached for the tray, and he handed it to me. How in the world was I supposed to ask him about it? "I was thinking about . . ." I slid the tray into a free spot in the freezer. *Just say it, Marybeth.* I busied myself with moving things around in the freezer. "I ran into Nick earlier."

"Nick Harker?" Like there was another Nick.

"Yeah." My heart beat hard as I shoved over a couple of frozen meals. "He came into my shop."

Luke said nothing, but I could feel the icy look I was sure had taken over his face.

I paused, drawing up the courage to repeat what he'd accused Luke of. Maybe I should just say it directly, stop trying to ease into it. "Were you in the car that fired those gunshots at the Harkers? Your senior year," I said as if this was something that had happened more than once.

Luke was quiet for a moment. I stayed where I was, letting the freezing air numb my face and my hands.

"Nick said that?" His voice was even.

I swallowed and finally shut the door. "He said he saw you in the car."

When I turned around, Luke was gazing at the wall, his hat on the counter and the remaining bags untouched.

I forced myself to speak past the fear of what I was afraid to hear. "Luke?"

He didn't look at me, but his jaw clenched and the bag under his hand made a rustling sound as he drew his fingers into a fist.

Oh, no.

Panic tried to claw its way up from my insides. I couldn't fall into it. As much as I wanted to scream and yell and cry, I had to stay calm. "Luke, please tell me it's not true."

He looked at me then, the older brother I'd always looked up to. The one I'd always run to for help or advice. The one I took care of when he couldn't take care of himself. He was still there, but his expression had gone flat and hard. "I could tell you that," he said slowly. "But it would be a lie. And after everything you've done for me, I can't lie to you."

A rush of breath escaped my mouth and I leaned against the fridge to keep from falling on the floor. It felt as if the house had imploded inside me, the dust and splintered wood and familiarity blowing up into something entirely unrecognizable.

"You didn't . . . You couldn't . . ." *You wouldn't actually shoot at my best friend? At* anyone? I couldn't finish the thought out loud.

"I wasn't the one holding the gun," he said.

I pressed a hand to my heart, thankful for at least that much. But I was angry. *So* angry, and it was beginning to well up inside me. "How could you? Luke, what if someone had died? What if Larkin had been shot?"

He rubbed a hand over his hair, making the sandy ends that curled around the edges stick out. I used to make fun of him for that, calling him a giant Gerber baby. Beneath the anger, an ache twisted like a knife.

Nothing would ever be the same between us.

"I didn't know what would happen," he said quietly. "There were some guys working for Dad. Not on the ranch."

There was a heavy silence between us as he waited for me to acknowledge what he'd said.

"What do you mean?"

He gave me a look that was almost pitying. "Come on, Marybeth. You knew what was going on."

I shook my head slowly. His words were almost an echo of Nick's, but somehow these hurt more. He'd lied to me. They *all* had.

"No." Maybe if he took the words back, they'd disappear into the ether and everything would be right again.

He just kept looking at me, waiting for me to come to terms with it. With the whispers I'd heard behind closed doors. Dad disappearing in the middle of the night. The strangers I'd told myself were there for ranch business. Everything I'd ignored or brushed off, because it wasn't something I could wrap my mind around as a kid. Every little clue I made myself too busy to pay attention to.

With a crashing realization, I knew what he meant. And even now, after keeping it from me for years, he couldn't name it. It was surreal, like I'd lived my life in this protected bubble, blissfully walking around assuming we were good and the Harkers were bad. It was all black and white back then, and where patches of gray had peeked out, I hadn't let myself see them.

I'd been okay with that, shoved it into the recesses of my memory. Until now.

"I know what you mean," I said, an edge to my voice. I felt exhausted, worn out by the years and years of a carefully constructed, so-called *good* family. "Tell me about these people who were working for Dad."

He eyed me carefully, as if he were afraid I might start screaming at him. "Some of them were around my age, and I started hanging out with them sometimes."

I vaguely remembered that, although at sixteen most of my focus had been on my own life. And whether putting all my attention on little dramas at school, Larkin, and admiring Gabe from a distance and wishing he'd notice me was just normal teenager stuff or purposeful distraction, I didn't know anymore.

"And," I pressed.

"They said they were going to scare old man Harker. They invited me along. It sounded fun."

I let out a short laugh.

A look of pain crossed Luke's face. "I've relived that night a hundred times, thinking of all the ways it could've gone wrong. I didn't *know* what was going to happen, Marybeth. I swear it."

"Did Dad send them?" I was feeling brave. How many more surprises could I take and still remain standing?

Luke shook his head. "Wasn't his idea. He didn't find out till after. And I paid for that, let me tell you."

I didn't know if I was grateful that Dad hadn't orchestrated it, or angry that my entire family had been lying by omission to me for so many years.

Luke ran a hand over his face as if this conversation was wearing him out. "Why the hell did Nick Harker bring this up now? And to you?"

"He wants me to tell Gabe. Apparently he never did."

Realization dawned on Luke's face. He gave a rueful smile. "Guess we have something in common, then."

I clenched my fists at my sides. I wasn't going to play into that trap. I didn't need to hear about how everyone was against my relationship with Gabe—again. And Luke wasn't sliding out that easy, leaving me feeling bad for something he did. I still didn't have all the answers I needed. "Nick doesn't trust you. He thinks that because of what you did back then, you've still got it out for him and his family. Including Gabe."

Luke raised his eyebrows. "Really?"

"That was the gist of it. So, do you?"

He stared at me a moment, and I expected him to say, *No, of course not. That's crazy.* But instead, he leaned back against the counter, resting both his hands on it.

"Nick thinks I'm the dangerous one. He tell you what he and Jackson did? After his father came over here, yelling threats and demanding Dad own up to what we did?"

I'd only heard about Mr. Harker showing up in whispers when I'd come back from visiting Larkin one night. But I knew what Luke meant. "He did."

Luke pushed himself up and paced across the kitchen. "That was the worst pain I've ever been in. Physical pain," he amended, and my heart constricted. He grabbed a bottle of water from the counter, but he didn't open it. "They're animals, Marybeth. The lot of them. You wonder why I can't stand seeing you with Gabe? That's why, and it's only part of it. We might have shielded you from a lot of what was going on, but you're smart. You know enough to know better. You should understand loyalty."

His words drew the breath from my throat. I struggled to find air under the accusation he'd thrown at me.

"That's not fair," I finally said, my voice tremulous and breathy. "And you didn't answer my question."

He held my gaze for a moment, and all I could think was that the brother I knew looked like someone else. "I can't answer that because I don't know."

I wrapped my arms around myself as Luke grabbed his hat from the counter. He pulled it on and crossed to the door before pausing.

"If Nick Harker comes back to your shop, you tell me." He turned then, his face like stone. "If he so much as looks your way, you tell me. And if that boyfriend of yours puts one toe out of line, tell him he won't be standing for long."

He left then, the slam of the door making the glasses and plates rattle in the cabinets. I fell back against the fridge, pressing my hands to my face.

Everything had changed so fast. I wanted it to go back, back to what I thought was normal and okay.

But the fact was, nothing was okay, and it never had been. I just didn't know.

I had to tell Gabe about Luke. How, I didn't know, but I had to do it before Nick did.

I owed him that much before I broke his heart.

Chapter Twenty-two

Nick

I DUG OUT A five and dropped it into the tip jar at the hot dog stand across the road from the motel.

"Thanks, man." The guy gave me a genuine smile, and I smiled back.

Sometimes Bent Creek wasn't all that bad.

I glanced at my phone. Gabe was due here in a couple of minutes. I'd played off Marybeth's quick retreat last night, distracting him with contact information for the lawyer's office that was serving as the registered agent for all those LLCs. It was too late to call then, so he'd suggested coming by today. He was a much better businessman than me. I planned to let him make the call while I stood by ready to look up whatever information he might get.

Across the four-lane highway, the motel parking lot was quiet. Only a few vehicles littered the lot at this time of the day. I stood against the door to my room and ate the hot dog in three bites while I waited for Gabe.

Minutes ticked by. I passed them with rereading texts from Larkin, whose number I'd finally gotten. She hadn't sent anything new this morning, so I typed out a quick message.

Hey. Thinking of you. Walk you to your car after work again?

A second ticked by. Two. Ten. Thirty. She was probably busy at work. She'd said it felt like business had been picking up at the coffee shop over the past few weeks, and if it was anything like that rush I'd seen in there the other day—

Sure. Off at 4 today. With a little smiley face emoji.

I grinned at the little yellow face. *See you then.*

If I played my cards right, went slow like she wanted, maybe that would turn into dinner sometime soon. Maybe she'd agree to let Diego join us, although I knew she'd take her time on that. Right now, I was still Mr. Nick, that nice guy who helped his mommy out once by taking him to the park.

I almost laughed at the thought. Never before had I pictured myself playing dad to a two-year-old. But, man, I loved that kid as much as I loved Larkin.

My thoughts stopped in their tracks. Did I mean that? I said it to her in high school, and I thought I'd meant it then. But I didn't know then what it meant for real.

I did now.

I grinned at the asphalt and my truck. I did love her. This didn't bode well for me getting out of Bent Creek again.

Before I could think about it anymore, Gabe's truck came flying into the parking spot next to mine, bits of gravel spewing out from under the tires when he braked. The door slammed when he got out, the noise instinctively setting me on edge. I shoved my phone into my pocket and braced myself when I saw the scowl on his face.

Marybeth must've talked to him.

"Hey," I said as I turned to unlock the door to my room. I pushed the door open, but Gabe stood rooted to the cracked sidewalk.

"Why are you here?" he demanded.

I glanced at the door to the shoddy motel room and played dumb. "I needed a place to stay?"

"In Bent Creek." He shook his head. "Forget it. I won't get a straight answer from you anyway."

I tucked my thumbs into my pockets. A seed of remorse was sprouting deep down inside, but I couldn't change the past. "Look, I'm sorry. I should've told you about Luke Noble back then. I thought I was doing you a favor, keeping you out of it."

"I don't care about then. I care about *now*."

I gestured at the open door with my chin. "You want to talk inside?"

His scowl deepened. "What I have to say won't take that long."

Glancing around the mostly—but not entirely—empty parking lot, I frowned at the thought of who might be overhearing.

"This place caters to methheads and truckers look for a cheap night's rest. No one here cares about us."

Fine. We could air it out in public, if that was what he wanted. "First, I didn't realize Marybeth didn't know when I mentioned it to her. And second, you needed to know so you could . . . make the right decision." I cringed inwardly at the phrasing.

"The right decision," he said, echoing my words, and I couldn't hide the wince this time.

Gabe threw up his hands. "Just admit it. You made it clear you hate the idea of me and Marybeth together. And you didn't come here to help me; you came to break us up. Because I can't think of any other reason why you'd bring all this crap up from the past now."

I dropped my hands from my pockets and clenched them into fists. He wasn't taking this seriously, and that was really bothering me. "I don't want to see you wind up dead."

He shook his head, his face filled with disbelief. "By who? Luke Noble? You know that guy's been mourning his dead wife for two years, right? And that Marybeth's a grown-up who can make her own decisions? He's not a threat."

"You're giving him too much credit."

"And you're perpetuating a war that ended when Pops went to prison. The Nobles won, Nick. They don't care anymore." He looked out at the parking lot, and I could tell he was trying to calm himself down. I almost wished he'd take a swing at me. Maybe it would clear his mind, make him see the truth.

"Did you have any interest in the ranch at all? Or did you just come here to destroy everything I'm trying to build?" Under the anger was a note of sadness, and it wrenched my heart.

"At first? No," I said honestly. "But now . . . yeah. Against all my better judgment, I want to know what's going on as much as you do. I want that land back."

He didn't say anything.

I took a deep breath. He wanted more, so I'd give him the truth. "Look, you're right, okay? I came here to put an end to you and Marybeth, because I couldn't—I *can't*—see a way it can work. And you weren't there that night. You didn't see him in that car, watch as he and his friends fired at our family, at my girlfriend, at me." I closed my eyes a second. "I'll never forget that moment as long as I live, Gabe. It's burned into my mind. If he did that then, and it took him no time at all to threaten you again, it's just a matter of time."

"He told Marybeth he wasn't the one who shot."

I shook my head. I didn't know. When the bullets started, I'd squeezed my eyes shut, pressed myself against Larkin, and prayed. "It doesn't matter. He was there. He was part of it." I paused. "Look, it's up to you. Maybe I came here on a mission, but I'm done with it now. You have all the facts, and you can decide for yourself. And whatever you decide, I'll respect it."

He frowned, looking off into the distance before dragging sad eyes back to me. "What I want doesn't matter. Marybeth already decided for me. I hope you're happy, Nick."

I didn't expect that. But I should be happy. I'd gotten what I wanted, hadn't I? Then why did it feel like I'd destroyed my brother's life? And why did I feel like a selfish jerk?

"I've seen you making an effort lately," he continued, his voice quiet as he studied the dead weeds and the salt lines in the sidewalk cracks. "Around town. Reaching out to talk to folks who looked at you in suspicion. Helping out. I thought things were going well, that maybe . . ." He looked at me then, pity in his eyes. "Maybe you should've started with your own family. Or was it all for show?"

"It wasn't."

He huffed, shaking his head. "Nothing you do would surprise me now. You could've taken a detour out to California to argue for parole for Pops, and I wouldn't blink an eye."

His words hurt. I crossed my arms and set my jaw, waiting to see if he had anything else to say. When he didn't, I finally spoke. "I did what I thought was best. You can take it or leave it."

Gabe stared at me a moment, then turned and strode back to his truck. The engine started, and then he was gone.

I dropped my arms, looking out over the asphalt and the dirty snowbanks piled around the parking lot.

I came here to save Gabe. I succeeded—and managed to lose the only real friend I'd ever had.

Chapter Twenty-three

Larkin

I'D JUST POURED A post-lunch dark roast for Emily Foley, the town librarian and Mrs. Foley's daughter, when my phone buzzed in my pocket. My heart lurched, the way it did every time I got a text now. I waved to Emily and hoped it was Nick, sending me something to make me smile—or anyone other than my text stalker.

I held my breath as I lifted up my phone. Marybeth. A whoosh of air exhaled from my mouth as I leaned against the counter to open the text.

I talked to Gabe. I frowned at the words, wishing she'd type faster. Surely Gabe would see that this vendetta Nick thought Luke had against him was ridiculous. To be honest, it didn't sit easy with me learning that my best friend's brother, the guy I'd joked around with and run errands for to help Marybeth, was with the people who'd tried to kill me back in high school. But I had only two choices: be angry with him and afraid of him, or believe what he'd told Marybeth when he said he didn't know what he was getting into.

I'd opted for the last one. I could've lived the rest of my life not knowing, and I'd never felt threatened by Luke. Ever.

I just wished I could get Nick to see that.

Marybeth's text came through, a barrage of words on my screen. I read through it once, then again, but the last lines never changed.

I can't fix it. I told him I needed a break.

My heart sunk. Nick told me he wanted Gabe to make the decision, but this wasn't Gabe. It was Marybeth, and I couldn't figure out what she was thinking.

No, what? Why?! My fingers raced across the screen.

It's not going to work. Luke hates it so much. You should've seen his face when I asked him if he'd ever go after them. He was like a whole other person. I've never seen him like that.

A few seconds passed as I thought about what to say.

Another text popped up from Marybeth. *If anything happened to Gabe because of me . . .*

My heart shattered for her. This wasn't right, none of it was right. They were so happy, and now . . .

I wish I could fix this for you. If only I could go back in time, find out what Nick knew, and stop him from saying anything.

She sent a heart emoji, and I replied that I'd stop by after work with Diego. Maybe then I could see Luke for myself. I just couldn't believe he'd act like that. Sure, he never liked the idea of Gabe and Marybeth, but he seemed to tolerate it.

And he certainly never acted like he'd do anything to Gabe.

Maybe if I talked to Nick. Convinced him that he'd made a serious mistake. Maybe there was something he could do to fix it. After all, he was the one who'd gotten into Marybeth's head.

It made me wonder if . . .

A couple visiting from one of the ski resorts stopped in, derailing my thoughts. But when they left with their coffees, I opened my texts again. Pulling up the ones from the text stalker, I re-read them.

Was this what that anonymous texter meant by showing me why Nick was really in town? To break up Marybeth and Gabe? It felt off, like it was too easy. I'd known for a while that he hoped that would happen. He'd even tried to get me to help.

My phone buzzed in my hand, and I looked down. A new text had popped up, like the anonymous person knew I was thinking about him.

This time it wasn't words, though. It was a picture. Or—I squinted at it as I tapped to open it. A screenshot, from some county jail website in Texas.

Nicholas Lane Harker. Possession with intent to deliver controlled substance, 1ˢᵗ offense.

I sucked in air as my eyes traced the words again. The image cut off his photo, but there was no mistaking the dark hair that showed at the bottom of the image.

Another text popped up below, another screenshot. This one was an email. The addresses and subject line were cut off, but the substance of the email was there.

Hi Felix,

Getting back to you about Nick Harker. His employment was terminated at the Triple Diamond due to arrest and incarceration on drug charges.

Unless you've got a soft spot for hard luck cases, I'd steer clear of this one.

Chris

My fingers trembled as another text arrived, this one a photo. A mug shot, probably the one missing from the first screenshot. Under the sullen expression, the swelling on one cheek, the black eye, and the longer hair hanging in his face, it was undeniably Nick.

"What did you do?" I whispered under my breath as I stared at the image.

Is this enough? I've got more.

The words taunted me, and I wanted to throw my phone against the wall. If it shattered, I couldn't see the picture, the information, the texts—none of it—anymore. I wouldn't have to know.

But I did.

Put it together, Larkin. You know what his family did for a living. You heard the gossip about him. Now you saw what he was up to in Texas. Why do you think he's here?

I squeezed the edges of the phone, not wanting to believe it. Not Nick. Not the guy I knew—that I'd *known*—for so long. He was honest with me back then, I thought. He'd fallen onto the wrong path, and gotten out. Stayed clear of his dad's business.

In case you're too slow to figure it out, here it is in plain English. He's here to rebuild what his father let fall apart.

He's not. I wanted to scream the words at my phone. Hit the call button and make this coward actually speak to me and hear the truth.

A word of advice. End it. Or you'll find yourself without your son.
He'd be better off anyway.

Bile rose up my throat. I dropped my phone and leaned my hands against the counter as I looked at the ground, willing my stomach to calm down.

Breathe. I had to breathe. In and out.

I stayed there as the minutes ticked by.

When I finally stood up, the world spun before my eyes. I grabbed hold of the counter. I couldn't face Nick, not yet. I needed someone else to look at those texts, talk me through this. Not Mom—she wished Nick would drive right back to Texas every day. It had to be Marybeth.

I shot off a quick message to Charlie, feigning dire illness, and locked up. Sonia would be in to relieve me in a couple of hours anyway. Despite what Charlie thought, the town of Bent Creek could live without their coffee for two hours.

And then I headed out of town, toward the Nobles' ranch.

Chapter Twenty-four

Marybeth

I blinked in the late winter sunshine, feeling like a flower that had come up too early in the season. Being in the park with happy kids yelling and laughing all around me was strange. After so much had changed, it felt like a place where I didn't belong.

Glancing at Larkin, it was clear she felt the same way. She gave Diego an empty smile when he showed her the rock he'd found. He scampered back to the little kids' climbing structure, and Larkin wrapped her arms around herself, almost disappearing into her coat.

"When are you going to see him?" I asked, carefully watching her to make sure she knew I was offering support and not pushing.

"Tonight."

My shoulders relaxed a little. At least she wasn't putting it off. I knew better than anyone that facing up to what had to be done was better accomplished sooner rather than later.

"Is it crazy if I believe there's somehow an explanation for all of this?" Larkin turned to me, her dark eyes full of hope.

I wrapped an arm around her and squeezed. "It's not crazy. You care about him. Of course you want all of this to be something the texter made up."

"I love him," she said quietly as she pulled away. "That's really crazy, isn't it?"

I rolled my lip between my teeth. "You feel how you feel. There's nothing wrong about that." But after I spoke, I thought for a moment. Did I think that after all that stuff the texter sent, Larkin was better off without Nick in her life?

I did. But I wasn't about to say that. Not when I'd been skeptical of him from the beginning. I'd held on to the power to make my own decisions about Gabe. She deserved the same when it came to Nick.

"You loved Gabe, didn't you?" she asked, her eyes on her son as he crawled over a plastic obstacle.

It was like pins stabbing at my heart. "I still do."

"Are you sure you did the right thing?" I could feel her watching me now, and I kept my own eyes on Diego.

"Honestly? I don't know. I miss him so much. But he's safer this way . . ." If anything happened to Gabe because of me, I'd never be okay again.

"What does he think about that?"

I shrugged, even though I knew exactly what Gabe thought. "Why are we talking about this again?"

"To get my mind off of talking to Nick. And those texts." She shuddered under her coat.

"Don't worry about what he—or she—said about Diego. Even if they did call Child and Family Services, what would they find? A mom and a grandmother who'd do anything for a little boy?"

"They'd ask about Nick."

"Larkin." I put a hand on her arm. "Stop. Talk to him, find out what's true and what's not. And go from there. And in my opinion, *there* means go to the police. I know I said that probably nothing would happen, but . . . just in case."

She took a deep breath, her gaze flicking to Diego and then back to me. "Yeah. You're right. Nick, and then the police."

I nodded, glad she was finally going to do something to put a stop to the texts. I was over this sick person torturing my best friend. I hoped they found him and put him away for a long time.

"Good," I said. "Now we should only talk about fun stuff. Like Diego and whatever mess he's making over there." I pointed at Diego, who was hard at work on something that looked like a mud pie.

"Oh, no," Larkin groaned.

"Okay, maybe not that. How about Bent Creek Spring Days? Can you believe someone nominated Kylie Young to head up the planning committee?"

"Homecoming Princess," Larkin added with a giggle.

I laughed too, and it felt good, even if it was over Kylie and her ten-year-long obsession with being Homecoming Princess—not even Homecoming *Queen*—our senior year. I was pretty sure she even had it on her resume.

"I need to get Diego home for dinner," Larkin said after we'd thoroughly discussed the Spring Days committee and what Kylie would do to it. It was exactly the distraction I'd needed from everything that had gone wrong in my life.

"Okay, let me know how it goes?" I didn't want to say Nick's name out loud and ruin the mood.

She nodded. Her phone buzzed as she took Diego's mud-covered hand. Fishing for it, she pulled it out as we walked toward the park gate.

Then she stopped suddenly.

"Larkin?" I turned around to check on her.

She was staring at her phone, and then, slowly, she held it up so I could see the screen.

I'm losing my patience. He was at the coffee shop today. You haven't ended it like I told you to.

Another buzz, and a second text popped up. *You have until noon tomorrow before I follow through.*

"Larkin." I held her gaze until she finally nodded.

"Nick," she said in a tight voice. "And then the police."

"Do you want me to come with you?"

She shook her head and pushed her phone back into her pocket. "I can do it."

"Okay." But as we walked, I didn't feel okay. Not about the texts. Not about Nick. Not about Luke. And not about what I did to Gabe.

Maybe I needed to have some conversations of my own.

Chapter Twenty-five

Nick

WARD WAS THE LAST person I expected to hear from as I was getting
ready to meet Larkin.

What's going on with Gabe?

Aside from getting dumped and probably wishing me dead? I
didn't know what my brother was talking about. Ward was the middle
one, full of obnoxious charm and good at getting his way.

*He's been after me to come home. Wasn't going to, but now he's telling
me not to. Are you down there?*

I went with the easiest, most obvious answer. *Marybeth broke up
with him.*

That's it?

Then, *you sure?*

I stared at his words for a moment. I'd been less than honest with
Gabe, thinking I was protecting him, and look where that had gotten
me. Ward was a grown man—he could take hearing about it. Maybe
it was time I stopped keeping it all to myself.

Mind made up, I typed out a response.

There's more. I'll tell you later.

I set the phone down and stared at myself in the mirror for a moment. I half expected to see a physical change as a result of all the other changes I'd been forcing on myself. Being honest with my brothers. Making an effort to show the people in this town that my family—that *I*—wasn't a monster. Finding myself genuinely interested in getting the ranch back.

But I frowned as I ran Ward's words through my mind again. I'd acted like Gabe and Marybeth breaking up wasn't that big a deal. I'd gotten what I came here for. But I wasn't sure if it was really what I wanted—or what was best—anymore.

Sure, I didn't trust Luke Noble. I never would. But I couldn't shake the feeling that I'd misjudged his sister. I expected Gabe to be the one to call things off, but Marybeth surprised me. I didn't think she'd put his safety first. Then I saw her through the window of her shop earlier, and she looked like a ghost. And Gabe refused to talk to me.

Gabe might be safer without her, but he wasn't okay. And as much as I tried not to care, Marybeth wasn't either.

Was it better to be safe or happy?

I didn't know the answer.

I frowned at myself and tried to focus on Larkin. She seemed to have forgiven me for my part in the Gabe and Marybeth mess. I left the motel with thoughts of her smile, the scent of her hair, the taste of her lips at the top of my mind. I couldn't drive fast enough to get to her house.

It was dark by the time I got there. I pulled up alongside the road, and idled there while I texted her. I didn't dare pull in the driveway, not after the last run-in with Jeanine. For all I knew, the woman would come storming out with a pistol the next time I stepped foot near her door.

A sliver of light came from the side of the house as the door opened. Larkin slipped out, a dark shadow in the porch light. I smiled as she approached the truck and jumped out to open her door.

"Hey, you," I said as she went to sit down.

"Hey," she said shortly. And instead of turning and reaching up to kiss me, she sat and pulled her purse into her lap. Her mouth was a straight line, and she didn't meet my eyes.

The anticipation I'd felt upon seeing her dissipated into a gnawing feeling of unease.

I rounded the truck and slid back into my seat. Resting my hands on the steering wheel a moment, I turned to Larkin. "Where do you want to go? We could go bowling. Or to the Rattlesnake. Unless you're hungry? Or we could go make out under the water tower." I waited for a smile on that last one, but Larkin just pulled out her phone and began spinning it around in her hands. "Or go bowling," I said again, that uneasy feeling growing.

"Can we just sit here a minute?" she finally said.

"Sure, if that's what you want." I drummed my fingers on the wheel, nervous energy forcing its way out.

"I have to show you something," Larkin said suddenly after a long minute had passed. "And then I need you to be honest with me."

"All right." Every stupid thing I'd ever done in high school ran through my mind. Then every word I'd said or move I'd made since I came back. That time I'd hooked up with Sarah Moyer before I'd even met Larkin. The candy bar I stole from the convenience store at fourteen. Had I said something else to Marybeth the other day that I'd forgotten about? Or was it that year I'd spent working for Dad? Larkin had never asked for specifics about that, but I'd give them to her if she wanted to hear it.

"Tell me about this." She held up her phone.

A photo of myself stared back at me. A mug shot. She quickly flicked through two more images. A screenshot of an email from an old foreman. And then one with my name—and a third degree felony in the great state of Texas.

I looked up at her, and she raised her eyebrows. She was pissed.

"That was a long time ago," I said softly.

"Was it? How do you define 'a long time ago'? Because the person who sent this to me seemed to think it wasn't."

The person who sent that to her? Who the hell would dig up my old rap sheet and send it to Larkin?

Oh, wait, that was easy. Luke Noble.

"It was two years after I moved down there. I was twenty years old, lost, confused, and really angry."

"So . . . what?" She glanced at her phone again. "That decided to make you want to sell . . . I don't even know what."

"Heroin," I said, the word pulling at all the wrong corners of my mind. All the dark, shadowy places I never wanted to visit again. "It was what I knew. That and cattle. I tried cattle, but I was too restless then. So . . ."

She stared at me as if she didn't know who I was.

I closed my eyes a minute and tried to pull my thoughts together. "It was a bad decision. I think I knew that going in, but I did it anyway because I didn't care. I didn't have you anymore, I didn't have my family or my home. I had *nothing* and it hurt."

"You could've had me," she whispered.

"I know that now. I figured it out at some point afterward, but then . . ." I gestured at her phone. "It was a stupid move, and I got caught. I paid for it, and I never did it again."

"I don't know what to believe, Nick." She kept looking at me in that way, like I was going to throw something else at her. "You keep pulling out secrets, and I'm afraid of what's coming next. What else don't I know?"

I let out a huff of air. "Nothing. I'm an open book, Larkin. I'll tell you anything you want to know. You want to hear about working for my Pops? I'll tell you about every time I laid out my rage on one of the Noble boys. What about that time I got together with Sarah Moyer? I regretted that one. You want to know who I slept with in Texas?"

She flinched like I'd slapped her with my words.

"I'm sorry. I don't know why I said that." I ran a hand through my hair. I was angry, and I didn't have any reason to be. "I just want you to trust me." I nodded at her phone. "Look at the dates on those things. I'm telling you the truth."

She held my gaze a moment, and then looked at her phone. She flicked through the pictures one by one. "There aren't any dates."

"Then Google it. It's public record." I paused, a more urgent thought pressing against my skull. "Can I see that again?"

Wordlessly, she unlocked her phone and handed it to me. I glanced at the phone number. "What's that area code?"

"Seattle. I looked it up."

"Why would Luke have a Seattle number?" I muttered as I skimmed through the images again. Headlights flashed across from us, lighting up the cab of the truck as some neighbor arrived home.

"That's not Luke," Larkin said, drawing my attention back to her. "I have his number saved." At my curious look, she added, "I helped Marybeth with him a lot when he was . . . grieving. He's got a local number."

"He could've picked this one up somewhere."

"Are you listening to yourself? That's ridiculous. And why would Luke mess with me? He's like a big brother."

I cringed inwardly at that thought. "What do you mean, mess with you?"

Larkin pushed her lips together, then reached over and scrolled up on the text chain. I looked down. And saw exactly what she meant.

You're a terrible mother.

Drug dealer.

Stubborn and stupid.

He's here to rebuild what his father let fall apart.

End it.

You'll find yourself without your son.

My blood boiled, raging behind my ears, blurring my vision. "How long have you been getting these?"

"Since right after you got here."

"And you didn't *tell* me?" My teeth were on edge. I wanted to find this pathetic excuse of a man and rip him apart.

"Oh, that's rich, Nick. I didn't tell *you* something. *One* thing. Because I wanted you to feel at home here, remember the good times and not shove the past in your face." Larkin reached for her phone.

I let it go and grabbed hold of the steering wheel again. "This guy is threatening you, and you wanted to spare my *feelings*? That doesn't make any sense."

"Yeah." Larkin's voice went deadly soft. "A lot of this doesn't make any sense. I have to go."

And before I could respond, she'd slipped out of the car. I went to open my door, but the look she shot me told me I'd better think otherwise. Instead, I rolled down my window. "I'm going to find this guy."

She turned then and strode back to the car. Leaning down, she looked right in my eyes. "Don't you dare, Nick Harker. I'm going to the police in the morning like I should have done a long time ago."

"The police won't do anything."

She ignored me, turning on her heel and stalking back toward her house.

I slammed my hands against the steering wheel. I'd messed everything up. *Everything*. I didn't know if there was any coming back from this. But I did know one thing for sure.

I wouldn't let Larkin get hurt.

I'd find this guy if it was the last thing I did, whether she wanted me to or not.

Chapter Twenty-six

Larkin

Noon the following day came and went.

The days after passed in a haze. There were no more texts. No visits from Child and Family Services. And no Nick.

I must've made the text stalker happy. After all, I'd done what he wanted. Why he wanted it, I didn't know. I promised the police officer I'd talked to that I'd let them know immediately if I heard anything else. But I hoped I'd never hear from him again.

Nick knew enough to stay away, although I spotted him around town more than once. He said nothing, gave me my space. We hadn't officially broken up but we'd also never officially been together.

I didn't know what any of this meant.

I missed him so badly it felt as if he'd ripped off another piece of my heart. How much of it could possibly be left? Between Nick and Will, it was a wonder that it kept beating.

I'd looked up Nick's arrest in Texas, and he'd been telling the truth. The date was a little over eight years ago. I was relieved to see he'd been honest about that . . . but still angry he hadn't told me about it upfront. Between that and Luke's involvement in the shooting, I was wary. He'd been so earnest when he'd told me I could trust him, that there were no more secrets. But I owed it to Diego—and to myself—to be careful.

As much as it hurt to push him away, I had to do it.

I held Diego's hand as he bounced happily through the mall. Mom had taken one look at me last night and pressed a fifty into my hand. "Retail therapy," she'd said.

Since I'd had the day off, I took Diego to the mall up by the interstate. I'd spent half the money on a new shirt for myself and the other half on toys for him. His eyes were bright and shiny as he took in the aisles at the toy store, and I lost myself for a while in his happiness.

"Ready to go home?" I asked after caving and spending some of my own money on ice cream for both of us.

He nodded. I grinned and wiped a smear of chocolate off his upper lip.

The entire ride home, we played his favorite songs and sang at the top of our lungs. It was the perfect distraction—and the perfect reminder of why I'd halted things with Nick. Diego was everything to me, and I couldn't let him become attached to anyone I didn't think would be there for the long run.

Tears pooled in my eyes as I watched him shimmy in his car seat to the music. I'd hoped Nick was going to be that one. I swiped the unshed tears away with the back of my hand.

By the time we pulled into the driveway, I was singing again.

My phone buzzed as I turned off the car. I pulled it out, my heart racing. Would I ever be able to just read a text without feeling as if everything was going to explode? But it was just Marybeth, checking in on me and asking if Diego and I would like to come over for dinner.

I typed out a yes before opening the door. I'd just lifted Diego from his car seat and set him down when a truck pulled into the driveway behind mine.

"Wait a minute, bud." I took Diego's hand to keep him by my side as I shut the car door. I didn't recognize the truck. It had stopped at the end of the driveway, too far away to make out the driver clearly. All I could tell from where I stood was that the man was white and had lighter-colored hair. He looked oddly familiar. I squinted, trying to jog my memory.

But I didn't need to, because the second he stepped out, I knew him instantly.

"Will?" I stared at Diego's father in disbelief.

Will Boden eyed me for a minute, as if he wasn't sure who I was, then his eyes flicked to Diego, and he smiled. "There's my boy."

Diego pushed himself against my leg, and I shook my head at Will. *He doesn't know*, I mouthed.

Will frowned, and I bit back the words that were on my tongue. *Why would I tell him about you? You didn't want anything to do with him.*

I gestured at the door. "Come inside?" I wanted to get this conversation over with while Diego could be distracted with his new toys.

"Sure," Will said, his eyes on Diego.

Still holding my son's hand securely in mine, I opened the front passenger door and grabbed our bags. I shut the door with my hip and noted ruefully that Nick would have at least offered to take the bags. Will just followed us like a shadow. He was nice to look at, but at this point, I didn't know what I'd ever seen in him past that.

Maybe all I'd seen were my own desperate hopes.

I dropped the bags on the kitchen table and made quick work of getting the packaging off Diego's new toy cars and building set. Will hovered by the sink, and when I came back from setting Diego up with his toys in the living room, Will was still there, acting as if his one job was to keep the sink and counter occupied with his weight against them.

I stood nearby, closer to the fridge where I could keep an eye on Diego. "What are you doing here?" I didn't know where to start with him, and this seemed as good a question as any.

"I came to see my son." He looked awkward, crossing and uncrossing his arms. He didn't belong here, and he knew it.

"After three years?" I raised my eyebrows as I did the best I could to keep the annoyance in my words to a minimum.

"Is there a statute of limitations on fatherhood?" he shot back.

My mouth opened slightly. I hadn't expected an argument from him. Not from the coward who vanished without a word when I was just barely pregnant.

He straightened and rested a hand on the edge of the counter. "I'm sorry, I didn't mean it like that."

I nodded, even though his apology sounded as shallow as the rest of him. "So . . . what are you asking?"

Will turned and looked at Diego, who was zooming a toy car across the carpet. "I want to see him."

A vise tightened around my heart. It was too much to hope for, that he'd changed and wanted to be a father—a *real* father—to Diego. "Like right now? Or . . .?"

"More than right now." He'd turned back to me, his hazel eyes catching mine. I used to think they were intriguing, with the way they'd look green or brown depending on the light. But all I could think of when I saw them now were Nick's gray-blue eyes and the way they made me breathless with just one look. "I want to be his dad."

I drew in a breath and slowly let it out. This was big, and I had to move carefully. "That's going to take some time."

"What do you mean?"

I tilted my head. "You've been gone for years. He has no idea who you are. I can't simply toss him at you and say, 'Hey, Diego, meet your dad!'"

"So you don't want to tell him?"

"That's not what I meant. It's just . . . I don't want him to get hurt, Will. Please don't get me wrong. I'm glad you're here. I'm glad you want to do the right thing." I paused, pressing my lips together as I searched for the right words. "You're going to have to rebuild trust."

"*I'm* going to have to rebuild trust?" He gave me a disgusted look.

"Yes. You walked out on him. I can't let that happen again. I can't let him get hurt." I crossed my arms.

"Wow, Larkin. That's . . . that's something else coming from you." He shook his head.

"I'm sorry?"

He started across the room. "You got a bathroom I can use?"

It took me a second to register the change in conversation. "Yeah, sure." I pointed down the hall past the kitchen.

He left, and I sucked in a breath. How was this happening? I'd always sort of hoped Will would come back around and want to build a relationship with his son, but there was something . . . *angry* about him. I couldn't place it, and it didn't match up to the man I thought I used to know.

With a quick glance at Diego in the living room, I turned to the fridge and pulled out a pitcher of iced tea Mom had made yesterday. I grabbed a glass and poured myself some. After taking a big gulp, I decided to pull out a baking dish and a mixing bowl. Diego loved to help me make brownies, and we could bring them over to Marybeth's later. I really wanted to hear what she thought about Will's sudden reappearance.

A noise from the living room drew my attention away from the ingredients. I took two steps to see into the room.

The front door was wide open. But something else was wrong.

"No." The word ripped from my throat as I ran into the room. "Diego!"

He was gone, his new toys left scattered across the carpet.

I flew to the door just in time to see Will settle Diego into the backseat of his truck. "Will! Stop, what are you doing?"

He didn't answer. And I didn't hesitate. I ran down the front porch steps to the driveway. But Will was faster. He started the truck.

"Will!" I screamed, my voice tearing at my throat. I reached the truck just as he started to back out. My hand hit the hood as it slid away. "Stop!"

He didn't even look at me. He stopped on the street as another car laid on its horn. Then he shifted into drive and tore down the road toward town.

I ran to the end of the driveway, screaming Diego's name so hard that it felt like the syllables were tearing against my throat. Where was my phone? I had to call the police. I had to get into my car and go after them. I had to—

"Larkin?" Nick's voice yanked my frantic gaze from the road to his truck. He was right there, on the road. He must've been the one Will had almost run into. "What's going on?"

"Will." My breath was ragged, and I was just barely holding it together as tears began to stream down my face. I pointed toward town. "He took Diego!"

Nick's face grew hard. He leaned over and opened the passenger door. "Get in. We'll get him back."

Chapter Twenty-seven

Nick

THE SECOND LARKIN WAS in the truck, I slammed my foot on the gas. She yanked the door shut and somehow had the presence of mind to put on the seat belt.

Her face a map of fear, she gripped the dash as I squealed around the corner onto Main Street, turning where I'd seen Will's truck go.

I squinted through the windshield as he careened around the corner onto Fifth Street.

"Did he say anything about where he was going?" I asked as I hung a right onto Fifth.

"No. He didn't say anything at all. He went to the bathroom and the next thing I knew, he was outside with Diego." Larkin's voice was strained as she spoke.

"We'll get him back," I said with all the ferocity I felt inside. "Hold on."

She grabbed the dash again as I followed the truck onto Highway 97 toward the Summit Mountain ski resort. Will accelerated as the road straightened, and my speedometer crept up to a number much too fast for this road.

"I'm going to ease up to see if he'll slow down."

Larkin nodded, her eyes fixated on the truck ahead of us. I slowed, and the gap between us widened.

"Slow down," I demanded under my breath.

He didn't.

I had to accelerate or we were going to lose him. "Did you call the police?"

"No, my phone is in the house."

"Use mine." I grabbed it from the cupholder, quickly unlocked it, and handed it over to her while I kept the truck between the lines.

Larkin made the call, answering far too many questions. From what I gleaned, Will had shown up out of the blue and run off with Diego after saying he wanted to be part of the kid's life again.

When she hung up, she was quiet for a moment. Then she said, "Will acted like he was angry at me."

That was interesting. "Like how?"

"He was nice at first, but when I started questioning him, he got short with me. Like I had no business asking him about why he was suddenly showing up. Or telling him I wanted to ease Diego into spending time with him. He was really angry that I'd never talked to Diego about him."

"Of course you didn't." The guy thought he could waltz back in as if he'd done nothing wrong, then run off with Diego as if he had some right to him. I tightened my hands on the wheel. I wouldn't mind getting a minute or two with Will Boden to set him straight.

"I would have when he got older, but now . . . he's too young to understand it. When I said it would take time, Will said—" Larkin stopped abruptly as I slowed down to round a corner. The road was winding as it approached the mountains, but Will hadn't eased up on the speed at all.

"What did he say?" I asked as we rounded another bend.

"Nick."

I glanced at her. Larkin's eyes were wide. "What?"

"He said that I had some nerve making him take it slow with Diego. As if . . . as if . . ."

"As if you hadn't done the same." The pieces of the puzzle slammed together in my head as the tires squealed around yet another curve.

"He's the texter," she whispered.

I wanted to throttle him even more now. "We're getting Diego back, I promise you." I reached over and squeezed Larkin's hand before putting it back on the wheel. The guy was pushing ninety in between the curves, even as we passed slower-moving cars, and it took all my concentration to keep up and keep the truck on the road.

"Where are the police?" Larkin glanced behind us, but there was no one there.

"We're only about ten miles out from the resort." I gritted my teeth as I flew around an old-timer's pick-up. "He'll have to slow down then." Summit Mountain was always mobbed with people this time of year.

"What if he doesn't? What if he doesn't care?" Larkin's voice cracked.

"He wouldn't have run off with Diego if he . . ." I shook my head. I couldn't say it out loud. "He'll slow down."

A ninety-degree curve was barreling toward us. I heard the screech and the thump and the scraping sound, and then it seemed as if time slowed. I hit the brake, hard. The truck fishtailed over the road as I went into the curve.

But it was too late.

All I could think as I threw an arm out to protect Larkin was, *This was how my mother died.*

There was an ungodly screeching sound, and then everything went black.

Chapter Twenty-eight

Larkin

I JERKED AWAKE.

But I hadn't been asleep. Burning rubber assaulted my nose as I blinked. Nick was next to me, slumped over against the airbag.

The airbag. I pushed against it and leaned sideways, gasping as the pain hit. My chest. My face.

"Nick." My voice scratched against my throat as I touched his arm.

He didn't move, and my heart began to race. Oh, no. No, no, no. I fumbled with the seat belt, and the memories came plowing back into my mind with the force of fireworks. Nick driving too fast. Trying to keep up with . . . Diego.

Diego.

Panic welled up inside me. The seat belt finally gave, and I shook Nick's shoulder. He raised his head, blinking. Bits of glass from the shattered driver's side window littered his hair, the airbag, his shoulders. Thank God he was okay.

"Larkin?"

"I have to get . . . Diego." It was hard to catch enough breath to speak, but I was able to grab the door handle. It opened, and I ignored the pain as I stumbled out. I grabbed the door as my head spun. The dizziness passed, and I held on to the truck as I made my way around it.

"Larkin!" Nick's voice was accompanied by the sound of scraping. He must have been trying to get his door open. As I rounded the truck, it was clear the damage was all on the front driver's side. The fender had slammed into Will's back end. And in front of Will's truck, an SUV was sideways with one tire off the road.

"Diego," I whispered as I grabbed on to Will's truck.

"Wait." Nick's hands grabbed hold of my shoulders, and I jumped at the pain. My entire body felt bruised. With effort, I turned to look at him.

The side of his jaw was swollen and beginning to turn purple and pink. Bits of glass still littered his hair, and he sucked in a breath when his left arm twisted just slightly with me shifting my weight.

"Wait here," he said.

Sirens wailed in the distance as Nick moved past me. I wasn't waiting. I didn't care about Will or what he might do to me. I needed to see Diego. *Now.*

Nick paused on the passenger side of the truck and peered in through the window. Then he reached for the handle and yanked. Once, twice, but it wouldn't give.

"Locked," he said.

He moved forward then, around to where Will's truck met the unlucky SUV. I stumbled to the passenger side and held my hand up to the glass to see inside.

Diego was there, wide-eyed and alert, in the truck's second row.

"Diego." My heart swelled with gratitude, and I gripped the door to keep from fainting in relief. "We're getting you out," I told him. "I love you, bud. Don't move, okay?"

He nodded, his big brown eyes taking everything in. His tiny body was way too small to be without a car seat, but at least Will had had the sense to put him in back and do up the seat belt.

I didn't want to think about what could've happened otherwise.

Shattering glass made me jerk up. On the other side of the truck, Nick tossed aside the rearview mirror, which he must have used to break the glass. Reaching carefully inside, he undid the lock and opened the door.

Will was out cold. I held up a hand to the glass on Diego's side to let him know I was here. It wouldn't be long.

Nick hit the button on the door, but nothing happened. He hauled Will out, one arm locked around either side of him. Dumping Will unceremoniously on the asphalt, Nick climbed into the truck, heedless of any injuries he might have had. He reached out and unlocked the back door, and before I knew it, I was opening the door to pull Diego into my arms.

"Oh, my baby. My baby." I held him close as his little arms reached around me. Burying my face in his hair, I took him away from that truck, back around to the rear of Nick's. "I'm so sorry. Are you hurt anywhere?"

He shook his head, but he didn't let go. I didn't either. I didn't know if I ever would.

A thud sounded from up ahead, and I looked up to see Will standing, one hand holding Nick against the side of his truck. Blood trickled down the side of Will's face, but he seemed not to notice. He sneered at Nick.

I glanced behind us, down the road, where I could still hear the sirens. *Come on*, I begged them to move faster, before Nick got more hurt than he already was. I didn't know what had happened to the people in the SUV, and all of this was starting to unravel fast.

Clutching Diego to my chest, a hand on the back of his head so he couldn't see Will and Nick, I took a step forward. "Will, get off him. He's hurt!"

"Good." Will practically spat the word. He shifted his weight and grimaced. He was injured too, and all I could hope was that it was enough to keep him from harming Nick.

Nick was white as a ghost, the blood drained from his face as if he were about to pass out. But he lifted both arms and wrapped his hands around Will's arm with an audible gasp of pain. I didn't know if he was moving on adrenaline or if he was in shock or what, but he twisted Will's arm away and shoved him around, until Will was the one pinned against the truck.

"I know what you did," Nick said, straining for each word. "Larkin never owed you anything. And especially not now." He took a second to breathe, which was long enough for Will to push against him.

But Nick held fast, his face contorted in pain, and Will's energy was running out. He slumped back against the truck. "I'm his father. You can't change that."

"You walked out on your own son. What kind of father does that?" Nick's fingers dug into Will's jacket.

"I told her the truth," he managed to say. "Which is more than you ever did."

"Nick . . ." I didn't like where this was heading. The police were almost here. *Come on, come on.*

Nick glanced at me. The anger fell away, and all I saw in his eyes was something pure. Something I'd been searching for.

It was love.

I clutched Diego to me as he turned back to Will. "I could end you right here, but I deserve better. It took me a long time to realize that. But I've found it now, and I'm not letting it go."

He glanced at us again, and my heart stuttered. He meant me. *Us.*

"I don't know if she'll have me, but you're not getting her son. You hear those sirens? They're for you. I'll let the police take you away." Nick leaned in closer, and I had to strain to hear his next words. "But you'll never come back here. Unless you want to know why the Harkers have the reputation we do. You understand me? And just in case you forget . . ." He drew back his fist and hit Will square in the jaw.

I gasped as Will stumbled back against the truck and Nick let out a string of curse words while he braced his arm against his chest. The sirens were on us now, lights illuminating the mangled scene and officers swarming out. EMTs converged on Diego and me, and I let them lead us away.

But first, I looked back at Nick. He'd dropped his hold on Will, and his eyes were on me as an EMT began asking him questions.

He was here for me. For Diego.

But was it enough?

Chapter Twenty-nine

Nick

Everything hurt.

The EMTs wanted to load me into the ambulance, take me to the hospital. I let them poke and prod and clean the cuts. One of them said my arm was probably broken.

But all I could think about was Larkin.

I spotted her while one of the EMTs was trying to convince me to get on the gurney. "I'm fine," I said over my shoulder as I beelined for her.

I stopped as Jeanine approached. Someone must have called her. I didn't know who they would have called for me. At this point, Gabe probably would've hung up on them.

She gingerly hugged Larkin and scooped Diego into her arms. Larkin said something to her as the EMT called after me.

"Sir. Sir! You need to go to the hospital. That arm is broken, and it won't set itself."

I ignored them, because Larkin was looking at me now. Those wide eyes, that sweet face, that soft hair. I'd committed every line and freckle to memory years ago. I just hadn't realized how much better the real thing was.

She was here now. I was here. And I was going to fight for her.

She began walking toward me, and I met her halfway. She glanced at the EMTs behind me. "They really want you to go with them."

"Broken arm," I admitted.

"Seriously? Nick, you need to go."

"Later." I reached up and pulled a single piece of glass from her hair. "Are you all right? Diego?"

"We're fine. They checked us both out. I'm going to take Diego to the hospital anyway, just in case."

I nodded.

She swallowed and went to wrap her arms around herself before sucking in a sharp breath. "Everything hurts," she admitted.

I laughed just a little, which hurt too. "Yeah. Same. We're going to be bruised up pretty good for a while."

She smiled a little before pinching her lips into a serious expression. "I don't know how to thank you."

"You don't have to," I said quickly. "You never have to." I paused. "Larkin, I—"

She shook her head. "Not now, Nick."

"I need you to hear me out. I'll respect whatever you decide, but please, at least give me a minute."

She sighed, glanced back at her mom and Diego, and then finally nodded.

Honesty. It was all I had, and I knew it was all she wanted—all she needed from me.

"I didn't know a good thing when I had it, back then," I started. "The truth is . . . You're a piece of my heart, Larkin. You always have been. I'd run through fire for you, for Diego. I want you. I want your son to be mine. I want to be a family."

I'd said it. The deepest truth from the most vulnerable part of my heart. She could twist it, throw it back at me, ignore it—but I wouldn't take it back.

I'd never take it back.

She watched me, her mouth slightly open and her eyes wide and a little scared. I wanted to kiss away the fear. I wanted to make her realize that the only true, good thing in this world was love.

"I love you." It was the last thing I had to give.

She said nothing, but I knew she was thinking. She needed time, and I'd give her all she needed.

"Go be with Diego. I'll . . . I'll get my arm fixed up." I gave her a smile before turning back to the EMTs.

She might not have known it yet, but I'd never give up on her.

Chapter Thirty

Marybeth

I TURNED THE KEY in the lock. The wind bit less than it had, which meant it wouldn't be long until spring. I'd always looked forward to the warmer weather, but this year I was afraid it might also mean a drop in people shopping at a Christmas store. The shop was hanging on, but I needed customers to keep coming in.

Turning, I dropped the key into my purse—and then almost dropped my purse when Nick Harker pushed away from the nearby wall and stood in front of me.

"What are you doing out here?" I eyed his coat, his tilted hat, the brace on his arm that stuck out of his sleeve. "Were you waiting for me?" Luke's warning ran through my mind. *You let me know if he shows up at your shop again.*

But after everything that had happened, I didn't have the energy to indulge Luke's fear or Nick's anger.

"I was hoping I could talk to you a second," he said.

I glanced back at the door, wondering why he hadn't just come inside.

"Figured your brother had issued multiple warnings about me by now, and I didn't care to run into him today." Nick gave me a half-smirk as he held up his broken arm. "I'm not really in fighting shape yet."

He looked pathetic, his face bruised and covered in healing cuts, and he seemed to wince every time he moved. For as much as I'd been suspicious of his motives toward Larkin since he stepped foot back in Bent Creek, he'd worked awfully hard to prove me wrong.

I leaned against the wall of the building and crossed my arms. "What you did was really brave."

He shrugged—and winced again. "I don't give a second thought when it comes to protecting Larkin and Diego."

I had to give him that. I'd talked to Larkin a few times in the days that had passed since the wreck. She knew how lucky she was. And I had a feeling she just needed the time to process everything that had happened before she came to the conclusion I'd already formed—she and Nick were meant to be.

"If you're going to ask me about Larkin, I can't tell you anything. She needs time to think."

"I wasn't going to ask you about Larkin." Nick had always had that overly intense look to his eyes, and I found myself wanting to look away, to squirm out from under it and run home. But I forced myself to stay put.

"Then why are you here? Are you going to tell me that Luke's issued some kind of hit on you?"

He smirked again. "Like to see him try."

I rolled my eyes. "I've had enough of this. I don't know why you're so obsessed with the past, but I'm done with it. I'm trying to move forward." I took a step away, and he held out a hand.

"Wait, please. I . . . I owe you an apology."

That stopped me in my tracks. I looked up at him. "For . . .?"

"Gabe. I thought I was doing the right thing. I still think . . ." He closed his eyes a second, like he needed time to work out the words in his head. "I don't trust your brother. I don't know if that will ever change, but I'm sorry for the way things turned out between you and Gabe. I should've told him myself and kept you out of it."

I stood there a moment, letting his apology linger in the air. "Thank you," I finally whispered. It was nice to hear, even though it did no good now.

He shoved his right hand into his jacket pocket. "Look, Gabe can handle himself, especially now he knows what happened. It shouldn't affect your relationship with him. Would you give him another chance?"

I raised my eyebrows as I dug my fingers into the sides of my purse. "You're asking me—a Noble—to get back together with your brother? Me, the one you seem to think is some kind of spy for Luke."

"I was wrong about that." He stared at me with that intense look again, and I didn't know how Larkin could stand it.

"Okay. Um, could you stop looking at me like that?"

He blinked. "Like what?"

"Like . . . never mind." I was grateful Gabe was more relaxed. I'd never sit easy with someone looking at me like that all the time.

Gabe.

"I know what you did for him, breaking up with him to keep him safe. That was . . ." Nick pulled his hand from his pocket and rubbed his jaw, then seemed to think better of it as a flash of pain moved across his face. "It was good of you. And it was what I wanted at the time, so I didn't see anything wrong with it even though I wanted Gabe to be the one to make the decision. But he can hold his own against your brother, and I should've had more faith in him."

I swallowed. I hated the thought of it, but Nick was right.

"He misses you, Marybeth. It's tearing him apart. I can see that without even speaking with him. He was making plans for you two. An apartment, a life together."

My heart lurched. We hadn't talked about moving in together. I'd thought about it, of course. But I didn't know he had too.

"Will you talk to him?" Nick looked at me with pleading eyes.

I nodded, slowly.

"Good." He smiled at me. "Thanks."

He left then, one hand stuffed back into his pocket, and I found myself hoping Larkin would see the light. Because I had a really strong feeling that Nick Harker was turning into a decent guy.

I pulled out my phone and started a text to Gabe. Luke wouldn't be happy if we got back together, but I was tired of living my life according to the past. He would get over it, or he wouldn't.

But Gabe deserved to be happy. And I did too.

Chapter Thirty-one

Larkin

Every day that passed seemed like a gift.

Even if I was constantly popping Tylenol to keep down the swelling and pain from the bruises. That didn't matter, because I was able to cuddle my son. So much that he'd started squirming away from me the second I hugged him. It was okay, though. He knew how much I loved him, and for the most part, he was okay after Will had taken him. He seemed more upset about the accident than about being kidnapped, and I was thankful at least that Will had been kind to him for that short time in his truck.

Will was in the county jail, locked up and waiting for his next hearing. Charges were pending, depending on how permanent the injuries the woman in the SUV had received. I hoped and prayed every night that she'd be okay. I hated the thought of anyone else suffering because of Will's actions. But each day that passed came with better news, and it seemed—for now—that she might fully recover.

He finally revealed to the police that he'd been watching me for a while, but he decided to act when Nick showed up back in town. It was unnerving, to think of someone stalking me all that time. But at least it was over now.

I opened a bag of carrot sticks for Diego—a gift from Nick. He didn't give them to me directly, just like he hadn't with the flowers, the toys, and the other bags of food that appeared on our doorstep. But I knew it was him.

He'd texted me a couple of times, just to check on how Diego and I were doing. He didn't push the conversation, and I was grateful. But every time I saw him around town—and I saw him *a lot*—my heart grew warmer.

I'd spotted him—one-armed—helping a delivery driver unload boxes of food at the café on Main Street. He'd sent apartment listings to Gabe, which I only knew because Marybeth and Gabe were talking again and she'd seen the texts coming through on his phone. I caught him joking around with Charlie, who was half laughing and half petrified. The day after that, Charlie grudgingly suggested I come into work early and bake some muffins to sell. And yesterday, I stood in disbelief as Nick worked with the mayor to repair the broken bench outside the library—with his arm still in a brace.

Nick Harker was acting like a model citizen, and I couldn't figure out why.

So when I spotted him walking past the coffee shop, I dropped the rag I was holding and ran to the door.

"Nick!" I shouted, leaning halfway outside.

He stopped and turned, a lazy smile lighting up his face and a hammer in his free hand. "Good mornin', beautiful."

Those words melted me inside, but I forced myself to keep a straight face. "What are you doing?"

He held up the hammer. "Going to drop this off for Mrs. Foley. She wants to hang some pictures, but she can't find her hammer."

I had no idea where he'd gotten a hammer—after all, cheap highway motels weren't exactly known for supplying an array of tools for guests—but that was beside the point.

"Why?"

He wrinkled his forehead. "Why what?"

I couldn't leave the coffee shop, but I didn't want to be standing out here on the street for everyone to listen in. I stepped back and held the door open. "Come in."

He followed me, setting the hammer on a table. It was the mid-afternoon lull, so no one was inside. Thankfully.

I crossed my arms and looked at him. It would have been so easy to let myself get lost in those eyes, that slight curve to his lips as if he were teasing me without saying a word, the way his shirt fit him so well under his open jacket. I cleared my throat and forced myself to look up. "You convinced Charlie to let me bake. I sold out of blueberry muffins this morning."

"I never thought there was any other possibility." He gave me a lazy grin.

"Hmm." He was going to drive me crazy with his lack of explanation. "Okay, tell me what's going on. Why are you suddenly Mr. Bent Creek?"

He drew his eyebrows together. "I'm not suddenly anything. But if you're asking why I'm making an effort—why I've been trying to make an effort—it's because I've decided I'm more than my past." He studied me a moment. "At first, I thought I wanted to prove myself, but it's more than that. I want a future here, Larkin."

I swallowed. "You're staying?"

He held my gaze, and I felt myself falling . . . I snapped my eyes away, looking at the wall, the tables, anything but at Nick Harker.

"I want a future here with you and Diego. I made that clear before. I haven't changed my mind. I never will."

I swallowed. Like a magnet, his presence pulled my gaze back to him.

"You take all the time you need," he said softly. "I'll be here."

My heart ached. I wanted to run into his arms, let him soothe away my worries and replace them with hope.

He looked at me like I was someone worth cherishing. "I don't know how. I don't know why. But something about you and me changes everything. You're everything I ever needed, Larkin. You take away the anger. You make the past fade away. You fix me, and I can't let you go."

And in that moment, I stopped fighting. I fell entirely. I'd been pushing so hard to stay apart from him, to think through things slowly, to make sense of everything.

But maybe it was time to act. Maybe it was time to leap.

"No more secrets," I said, my voice shaking just a little.

"No more secrets."

"What if I don't need time?"

He said nothing. I think I surprised him.

"Nick, I love you." The words rushed out of me. "I don't know if I ever stopped. And it's terrifying to admit."

His mouth opened, but no words came out. Instead, he reached for my hand, and I let him take it. His thumb traced a soft line over the back of my hand, and it gave me courage.

"I love that since you came back, you've been there every time I needed you. I love that your heart is in that ranch on Quarter Mile Road. I love that you'd do anything to protect your brother, even if I didn't like the results. I love the way you've fought for me. And most of all, I love the way you are with Diego." I looked up from his hand to his face. "I love *you*."

He took his hand from mine and pushed that errant lock of hair out of my face again. It was the simplest, sweetest gesture, and I wanted him to do it over and over again.

"Are you sure?" he asked.

"More than sure." And I was. The doubts were gone.

"Then my entire, overly honest soul is yours, Larkin Reyes."

I laughed. "Just please—*please*—don't ever tell me about Sarah Moyer, okay? I can live without knowing those details."

He grinned. "You got it. But maybe you'd like to hear about that time Gabe and I swiped beer from Pops and—"

"Later." I closed the space between us, stood on my tiptoes, and wrapped my arms around his neck.

"Are you sure you're sure?" He gave me that annoying, adorable smirk.

"Positive. There's only one thing I want right now."

He lifted his hand and laid a finger against my lips. I was pretty sure it was the first time he'd *ever* stopped me from kissing him. I frowned with disapproval. "I have to ask you something first."

I sighed, but nodded.

"This is going to sound crazy, but hear me out. I'm going to ask you to marry me, Larkin. Not now. But soon. I just wanted you to know that."

I stared at him. He really was crazy. And I loved him so much, I thought my heart would burst. So I did what felt right.

I kissed him. I put every ounce of myself into that kiss. It was a thank-you, I-love-you, and you-are-everything-to-me kind of kiss. I held on to him as if he were my lighthouse in a storm, because he was.

He returned the kiss, just as hungry as I was, just as urgent. I pressed myself into him, dropping one hand to his arm, and he winced under my lips.

"Did I hurt you?" I said, pulling away. Half of his face was bruised. Of course I'd hurt him.

"Yes. No. I don't care." He pulled me back to him, and I went willingly, laughing until the heat of his mouth took my breath away.

The bell over the door jingled, and I didn't care.

But Nick, ever careful of my job, gently pulled back. "Soon," he whispered against my lips.

"Soon," I repeated.

Chapter Thirty-two

Marybeth

"Where'd they go?" Gabe paused next to me, his hand pulling me to a stop. He glanced behind us, back toward the café where we'd just had lunch with Nick and Larkin.

I followed his gaze, only to find my best friend and Gabe's brother locked in a kiss in the middle of the sidewalk, completely ignoring everyone around them.

Gabe shook his head. "You think they do that when Diego's around?"

"No, Larkin barely lets him come over. She's just started letting him stop by for an hour or so, because she doesn't want Diego to think it's more than he knows about yet."

Gabe raised his eyebrows. "It *is* more. He fully intends to marry her."

"I know." My mouth curved into a smile as I watched them. Larkin was so happy, and I wanted it to stay like that for her forever. "She's just very protective of her son. Nick's fine with it." I turned back to him. "Don't you guys talk about this?"

"Nope. We have an unspoken agreement not to get involved in each other's relationships anymore."

I supposed that was probably for the best. Gabe taking me back was the happiest day of my life, and I was perfectly fine if Nick stayed out of things from here on out.

"So what did you think of the place over by the B&B? The house?" Gabe asked.

"It had two bathrooms. And a garden in the back yard." With a back yard, I could have chickens.

"Did you break the news to Luke yet?" he asked. "Should I start looking over my shoulder?"

I groaned. I was *not* looking forward to informing my brother that Gabe and I were moving in together. "I'll deal with that when we sign a lease. There'll be no going back then."

Gabe's hand tightened around mine. A sure sign he was worried.

"Hey, he'll be fine. He'll deal with it. He's dealt with us getting back together. He has to know it's going to move forward."

"He hasn't spoken to you since we got back together."

I made a face at the ground. Luke wasn't dealing with it well, but he'd kept it to himself at least. And it wasn't as if I was striking up conversation with him after everything I'd learned. "It's my choice. He doesn't get to make it for me."

"All right. But I'll start looking at places in Mexico just in case we have to leave in the dead of night."

I looked up to find Gabe giving me a little smile. It worked. If he could make light of it, I could too. Maybe that was the best way to deal with Luke.

"Are they coming?" I looked back at Nick and Larkin again. Who were *still* liplocked in the middle of the sidewalk.

"Oh, for heaven's sake. Nick!" Gabe bellowed down the sidewalk.

He pulled away, finally, and they started toward us.

"What's going on?" Nick asked when they reached us.

"We were going to try to catch the movie, right?" I asked.

"Oh, right," Larkin said, her voice taking on a dreamy quality.

Gabe rolled his eyes at me again, and I covered a giggle with my free hand. Ahead of us, a small group that must have come from one of the resorts milled around outside the coffee shop. A woman in a long wool coat and heels darted between them, clearly on a mission of her own. Bent Creek felt lively, and it lifted my spirits even more. Maybe this coming summer wouldn't be so bad for my shop after all.

"Creason! Hey!"

Gabe stopped at the sound of his name. Just behind us, Kyle Clemmons came jogging out of his real estate office.

"Glad I saw you. Hey, Harker." Kyle and Nick bumped hands. "You just missed her." He pointed down the sidewalk, past the resort group.

"Who?" Gabe asked.

"Her name was Violet Barnes. She works for a company called Willow Cosmos, and she's looking to buy a ranch up by the interstate." Kyle looked from Gabe to Nick.

I made the connection at the same time they did. "It's another LLC."

Kyle nodded.

Nick ran out into the street and stood there a moment, before jogging back. "She's gone. Did she say why she wanted the ranch? Or where she was from? Anything?"

"I couldn't ask too much without looking suspicious," Kyle said, dropping his hands to the pockets of his khakis. "But I did get a picture."

"You sneaky little . . ." Nick started before laughing.

Kyle held out his phone. A fuzzy image of a woman with light brown hair, a pointed chin, and a serious look on her face filled the frame as she looked off somewhere to the right. She appeared to be about our age, and she clearly meant business with that tailored jacket and buttoned-up top.

"I'll send it to you." Kyle tapped his phone. "I told her I'd find out more about it. She didn't leave me a number, just said she'd check in again soon."

"That's weird," Larkin said. "Why wouldn't she leave her number?"

"Because she doesn't want anyone to know what she's up to," Nick said darkly.

"Or she's trying to hide her presence in town," Gabe added.

It sounded so out there. But with the little we knew about these companies, it seemed right.

"Let us know if she comes back?" Nick asked Kyle.

He nodded, and we continued down the sidewalk, skirting around the resort folks. Nick fell in next to Gabe, and I stepped back to walk with Larkin.

"We need to find her before she leaves town," Nick said in a low voice.

"She's going to lie low. She's probably already on her way out," Gabe replied.

"Then we need a new tactic. I can hire someone to track down that lawyer, the one registered with the companies. It's weird abut that number and address."

I'd helped them with that, paging through online maps only to discover that there was no building in existence at the address listed on the state's website. And the phone number hadn't been in service in at least three years.

"Maybe." Gabe went quiet. "We need help."

"Did you talk to Ward?" Nick asked.

I glanced at Larkin. She shrugged, as if she didn't know anything about it. I remembered Ward Harker. He was in our class, and he could've talked the venom out of a snake back then. He'd run one entertaining but unsuccessful campaign for class representative. And then he'd left at the end of that year, along with the rest of them, when their father was arrested.

"He won't come," Gabe said.

"Figures. Money's too good for him to leave it behind."

"What about Jackson?" Gabe asked. "He won't get back to me."

"Same. Worries me." Nick lapsed into silence after that.

Gabe glanced back at me and smiled. The worry I'd heard in his voice had disappeared, and I reached out my hand.

He stepped back to take it and gave me a peck on the cheek.

"Oh, please, get a room," Larkin shot over her shoulder with a smile as she moved up to walk with Nick.

I took one look at Gabe and burst into laughter. "You're one to talk," I said back to her once I could breathe again.

Gabe wrapped his arm around my shoulder and I sunk into his embrace.

"The ranch will work out," I whispered. "I know it will."

He kissed me again. "If it does, I plan to sit on that porch with you every evening."

"We might have to fight Nick and Larkin for that right."

He laughed. "Can you imagine? The four of us sharing that place?"

I didn't even want to see the look on Luke's face if I mentioned that. "We'll build our own," I said confidently. "No sharing."

"You've got a deal."

"What if you convince Ward to come back?"

"He'll have to fight it out with Nick. Which means he's building his own place too."

I laughed, imagining all these little cabins popping up on the Harker land. I glanced up at the fading sunlight, and then waved at Emily Foley across the street. "Bent Creek doesn't know what hit them yet, do they?"

I could feel Gabe's grin. "Not yet. The Harkers are back in town. For good."

Epilogue

Jackson Harker

"One phone. One wallet. Twenty dollars, license, debit card. A lighter. Smoking's bad for you, you know that?" The woman at the desk raised an eyebrow at me like a condescending mother.

"I don't smoke."

"Sure you don't. Sign here." She tapped the paper with a ballpoint pen.

I scratched off something that looked like my name and began collecting my stuff.

The woman turned the paper around and examined it. "Jackson Douglas Harker. You don't look like a Douglas."

"Family name," I grumbled. My phone was dead, of course. A useless hunk of computer chips and whatever else they stuck in those things to make them work.

"Well, good luck, Mr. Harker. And I hope to never see you back here at the Williams County Jail."

"You and me both."

Outside, the sunlight was blinding. I blinked into it, savoring the bleak warmth against the chill of the morning. It was spring, just barely. And for the first time in 120 days, I was living on my own terms.

My first stop in this pathetic little town was a convenience store, where I spent some of my twenty-five dollars on the basics, including a phone charger. My next stop was McDonald's, where I tore into the best-tasting Big Mac and fries while waiting for my phone to charge enough to use. As I chewed, I gave a side eye to the bar across the street that had gotten me in more trouble than I could handle a few months ago.

My phone, cracked screen and all, sprang back to life with a barrage of texts and notifications. Shoving the last of the fries into my mouth, I picked it up and glanced at the wall of texts. An old girlfriend. A couple of friends. An old colleague, if you could call him that. Some people I wished I'd never met. And my brothers.

Curiosity got the best of me on the last one, and I opened up that text string first. Skimming through, I got to the bottom with more questions than answers. Something about Gabe shacking up with the Noble girl, Nick wrecking his truck to get some stalker messing with his high school girlfriend, the ranch, Luke Noble, and a bunch of companies with nature names.

I stared at the last one a minute. *Anyone hear from Jackson?*

Guilt threatened to invade, but I shoved it away. I didn't have to answer to them for anything.

But as I crumpled up the packaging on the table, the guilt snuck in anyway. They were my family—all I had left of it. Least I could do was let them know I was alive.

I'm here. It was short and to the point.

I stood up and went to shove the phone into my pocket when it rang.

Nick.

With a resolute sigh, I answered as I pushed my way out the door. "Yeah?"

"Hey to you too." His voice was the same, low and slightly irritated. It made me smile anyway, and not a lot had made me smile at all in the past few years. "Where have you been?"

I heard the worry under his casual question. I knew him too well *not* to hear it. "Busy." I posted up next to the trash can outside the McDonald's, facing the mountains off in the distance instead of the bar across the road.

"Too busy to let anyone know you weren't dead?"

A lick of annoyance lit up inside me. Nick was the closest to me out of all my brothers, and the big brother thing didn't go over well these days. "What do you want, Nick?"

He let out a breath. "We need your help, Gabe and me."

I thought back to the texts. "Does this have something to do with the ranch?"

"Yeah. We hatched an idea, but we need someone to carry it through."

"So what, you need me as muscle or something?"

He laughed. "No, not like that. It'll make more sense when you see it. Can you get down here? Where are you, anyway?"

Closer than I'd like to be, I thought as I stared at the mountains. I had nowhere to go. No apartment, no job, no girl, nothing. What did I have to lose in Bent Creek that I hadn't lost already? "Sure. Shouldn't take too long."

Nick waited a minute, but when I didn't answer his last question, he went on. "All right. I'm at the Slope Motel, up by the interstate. And by the way, I'm going to ask Larkin to marry me. You're going to be a groomsman. Clean yourself up so she doesn't take one look at you and kick you to the sidelines."

He hung up, and I stared at the phone.

What had I just gotten myself into?

Thank you so much for reading! I hope you enjoyed Nick and Larkin's story—and meeting the Harker and Noble families. **Find out what happens next** when Jackson comes back to town and falls hard for Emily, the town librarian, in *A Bent Creek Redemption*. And if you haven't read Gabe and Marybeth's story, be sure to check out *A Bent Creek Christmas*.

Come home to Bent Creek... a small town in Montana where everyone knows everyone, secrets live in the shadows of the mountains, and love is waiting to be found. The Harker Brothers Ranch series tells the stories of six brothers—Gabe, Nick, Jackson, Ward, Colt, and Maverick—as they return with one goal: to get the family ranch back in their hands. Reckoning with their family's past, the Nobles, and each other, each one finds love and home again in their hometown.

Join my email newsletter at catiecahill.com to keep up with everything Bent Creek.

More by Catie Cahill

Visit CATIECAHILL.COM FOR A full list of Catie's books.

About Catie

CATIE LIVES WITH HER family in Kentucky but half her heart is in the Rocky Mountains. Catie loves animals, planning travels, reading, and spending time with her family. Visit her online at catiecahill.com.

* 9 7 9 8 9 8 8 5 5 0 9 1 4 *